SEALED IN

By

Jacqueline Druga

Sealed In
By Jacqueline Druga

Brief Introduction

Russian President, Boris Yelstin, when newly elected in 1992, publicly announced that the Soviet Union had retained an illegal offensive biological warfare program. He immediately signed a decree banning the development and research of offensive biological weapons. A repercussion of this ban would cause many Russian scientists in the biological warfare arena to seek work in other countries. Many of these scientists defected.

Sequentially, in 1992, Russian scientist and defector Ken Alibek attested that Russia had developed a hybrid of the Ebola and smallpox virus for use as a biological weapon, known as Ebolapox.

The hybrid would combine the devastating and hemorrhagic effects of Ebola with the highly contagious nature of smallpox. The weapon caused lesions to appear below the skin's surface; the skin blackens and peels away in layers. Mucus membranes disintegrate. What begins as common flu symptoms will in four days break down the body inhumanely, and death is inevitable.

Because of the combination, the weapon's fatality rate is near 100%. Alibek deemed it as the weapon that, once released into society, would inevitably come back to those who released it. Further researched was needed.

Then the program was banned.

It is conceivable that many of the Russian biological weapon scientists retained samples of the hybrid before defecting. It is out there in circulation. The Soviet Union highly refutes this rumor, yet has been unable to prove that all specimens of Ebolapox have been destroyed.

In 2002, a mysterious illness erupted in Pakistan claiming at least ten lives. The distinct similarities led scientists to believe it was the Ebolapox virus. Pakistan was not the first of these mysterious outbreaks, and until all of the weapon is eradicated, unfortunately, it will not be the last.

FLASH FORWARD

Ground Zero - 1

Hartworth, Montana

December 23

The wide eyes seemed to stare at Dr. Edward Neil, following him around the room like a painting. Eyes that were open, didn't blink, the color of them lost in the blood flow that had poured into the white portion of the eyeball and turned black.

The victim had to be in his twenties and he, like everyone else Edward Neil guessed that he would encounter in Hartworth, Montana, was dead.

The quiet, small town, nestled in the north of the state close to North Dakota and Canada, was an entity all to itself.

The nearest neighboring town was forty-three miles west.

It had been days since a car moved down the road or a person walked the streets

That's what Edward estimated.

They entered into the town alone in protective garb. A fresh blanket of snow lay upon the unmoved cars, covering the Christmas decorations that gave even more a depth of sadness to the situation.

The song, *Silent Night*, would forever hold new meaning. It eerily played on 'auto' through the streets of the town.

How fitting.

There were homes and ranches within the boundaries of Hartworth; those had to be checked, as well. But Edward felt it would be useless.

They would bring no one else into the town until he and his team had thoroughly gone through and confirmed what had occurred.

Edward hadn't a clue what killed everyone, not yet. Skin appeared as if it boiled below the surface, black as if burned, but it wasn't charred; it was blood. Skin peeled off in layers and adhered to the bedding. This more than likely occurred while the victim was still alive. It happened only after they literally vomited out their insides, and blood seeped from every orifice.

He stopped about five victims into his search and made his way to the utilitarian metal lab trailer set center of the one-stoplight town.

After disinfecting, he removed his garb and poured a cup of coffee. They'd only just set up, had not been in town that long, and already Neil felt the wind knocked from him.

He sipped his coffee. It made him sick. He had been in the field and worked for the CDC for years;

never had he seen anything as horrendous as Hartworth, and he'd barely scratched the surface.

When the call came about Hartworth, he was back in Vermont actually joking around with Dr. Walker about a zombie apocalypse. The odd timing of the call coupled with the conversation sent a chill up his spine.

Receiving only minimal details and a directive to pack a small team and go, Edward knew he wouldn't be home for Christmas.

It was strictly confidential. In fact, Edward had never encountered something as classified as this.

A small team would go into Hartworth; four CDC security squads would police the neighboring roads wearing gas company logos. The story was a gas leak.

Hartworth, like many small Montana towns, was an entity of its own, so it wasn't uncommon for someone from a neighboring town to go days or even weeks without having contact with Hartworth.

Because of that, Edward hadn't a clue when the outbreak occurred or how long they were dead. Those were part of the answers he had to discover.

The dead town, however, was luckily discovered by a keen state trooper, Steve Irwin, who had a cousin that worked as a secretary for the CDC in Atlanta.

The trooper was at a crossroads about six miles from town and thought it odd that at two in the afternoon, there were no car tracks in the snow, nor had any attempt been made to maintain or ash the roads out of Hartworth.

He needed only to make it to the edge of town, and he knew.

He discovered the first body in a pickup truck right at the beginning of town, decimated by illness. The young man held a shot gun and looked as if he were standing guard, or rather sitting guard.

Irwin took a picture of it with his phone, and before calling it in to the station, he called his cousin at the CDC. The trooper's slip in protocol was actually a good thing. It worked in favor of keeping the situation tight-lipped and secret.

The picture went through the CDC faster than any disease.

Irwin was told not to go into town, to report it as a gas leak, and position troopers on the outskirts to keep people away.

He did. Irwin and the other troopers immediately went into quarantine in a special CDC trailer.

As far as the story of the gas leak told to the State Police, Edward was still fielding questions regarding that.

Something he could handle.

What he couldn't handle was the daunting task of solving the mystery before him. He would with the others, bit by bit, piece by piece, body by body.

He had to do so quickly, because with something as deadly as what wiped out Hartworth, Edward was certain he didn't have much time.

But before he found the answers to what happened in Hartworth, he had one very important task to complete. First and foremost he had to find out if the bug crossed boundaries. If it did, the CDC had bigger problems to face than just one small dot on the map.

Chapter One

ONE MONTH EARLIER

Lincoln, Montana

November 28th

Stewart Burton could have been a starting quarterback for the Miami Dolphins. He almost was. They scouted him and wanted him. His college statistics were phenomenal. He had the talent, personality, and the good looks to endorse any product.

But two things stopped that from happening. Neither of them were an injury.

In his senior year, he found out his college girlfriend was pregnant, and his mother died, both occurring in the same month.

Not only did his state of mind wander from the game, but his father needed him at home. Stew could have gone on to play football, but his father and the ranch took top priority.

That was forty-two years earlier.

His father, in exchange for helping him on the farm, gave him a small piece of property. Stew bought two horses for the land. Eventually, with his father's passing he inherited the rest of the property.

He still farmed some wheat, but his primary interest was thoroughbreds.

And really, he didn't need all that land. He rented it out, even to his own daughter, who built her home a half a mile from him.

Stewart Burton was one of the two richest men in the county and in Lincoln, Montana.

Three things came out of Lincoln; pretty much everyone who wasn't working a business in town made a living producing or aiding in those three things.

Wheat, thoroughbreds and the best flannel shirts in the country.

Handmade … sort of. Ty-Bow Flannel. Tyler Bowman was the other richest man.

But neither of the two men, both who lived in Lincoln, acted like rich men.

Stew was as down to earth as they came. A strong man with a barrel chest, a man who used to be muscular and athletic, but his body kind of shifted the bulk in various places. His wife of thirty-some years died in her sleep six years earlier. Heart failure, he was told. Stew never remarried, nor would he.

He loved Lora and always would.

He wasn't lonely, not at all.

Aside from friends, Stew had a semi-sane daughter, two grandchildren, a great granddaughter, and his life was full.

He worked and lived his life for his family.

The day after Thanksgiving, Stew liked to go into town. He actually went into town every day, but Black Friday was his favorite.

Not that the shops and restaurants that spanned the three blocks of the small town offered great deals; they didn't. Because the town was empty on Black Friday, everyone went somewhere bigger to shop.

Stew also enjoyed watching the town maintenance engineer, Andy Jenkins, hang the Christmas decorations.

Andy wasn't bright, not at all, but a good fella. A nice looking kid, Stew would describe him, even though he wasn't a kid. Dark wavy hair that didn't gray and a rugged face. It was too bad he just couldn't convey his thoughts. He went to school with Stew's daughter Emma, and then just after high school Andy was in a motorcycle accident, suffered a major head injury, and was never the same again.

He picked up the streets of Lincoln, decorated for holidays, and Stew employed him as a stable hand, as well.

Andy was a nice guy, funny to watch and listen to. He spurted out his own G-rated cursing when he messed up. And that was often.

Stew heard him.

"Gosh darn, son of a gun! Fudge filled cheap buttock lights!" Andy blasted.

Stew laughed, looked up to Andy who stood on a ladder, his lanky body barely holding on.

"You okay up there, Andy?" Stew yelled.

Andy peered down, almost losing his balance. "Oh, yeah, hey, Mr. Burton. I'm … I'm … good. Just… just trying to find the bad b …. bulb."

Stew cocked back some. "Thought that was a thing of the past."

"These lights are from … from ... eighty-f…. eighty … fer…. 1970; trust me they are a thing of the past … the past."

Stew laughed, was impressed at Andy's quick wit, and after wishing him luck, headed into to Bonnie's diner. There were about six people in there, mainly men his age having coffee.

He took a seat in a booth, and Bonnie came over within a few seconds. Instead of placing down a menu, she set down a newspaper.

"Morning, Stew. Back from shopping?"

"You know I don't shop until the last minute."

Bonnie smiled, pouring his coffee. "Usual?"

"Yes, please, and thank you." Stew added the cream to his coffee and slid the paper into his view. The headlines weren't anything spectacular, but Stew would skim through them while waiting on his eggs and toast.

It was a quiet, peaceful moment …

"Pap!" Her voice yelled at the same time as the bell above the door dinged.

Stew, like two other men in the diner, looked up at the call of 'Pap'. He peered down to his watch when he saw his twenty-year-old granddaughter, Heather, plowing into the diner. It was only a little after nine. "What's wrong?" he asked her.

"Oh, nothing." After giving him a kiss to the cheek, she slid in the booth across from him. Her shoulder length brown hair was pulled into a sloppy ponytail and her bangs danced across her forehead.

"Then why'd you come in here screaming my name?"

"I'm excited."

"For?"

"I went shopping. I got so many bargains." She nodded proudly. There was a childlike aura to her, an innocence, even if she was beyond her teens.

"Good for you. Are you hungry?"

"Very. I need a menu." She peered around.

"No, you don't," Stew said. "It's breakfast, who the hell needs to look at a breakfast menu?"

"I guess you're right."

"Where's the baby?" Stew asked, referencing Heather's two-year-old.

"With Mom." She was antsy with excitement, almost childlike.

"Your mom took her shopping?" Stew asked. But before he could get his answer, Bonnie came over and Stew ordered for Heather. He then double questioned. "She took her out on Black Friday?"

Heather giggled. "No. Jeez. Mom's not shopping. She's …" she stopped speaking and shook her head.

"What?" Stew asked. "She's what?"

"She's in the hole."

Stew cringed. "Damn it, she has the baby down there?"

"Well, yeah, she says she wants her to get used to being there."

Stew sat back and closed his eyes. "Why do you let your mother do those things with the baby?"

"Because Mommy loves Cody. It makes Mommy smile and Cody likes it too. Besides, Pap," Heather sat up straight. "The seismologist guy called the other day. Said levels were rising. How do we know? We don't."

"You sound like your mother." Stew rubbed his eyes "Do I have to call the doctor again?"

Heather shook her head. "No, she seems pretty stable. Just doing inventory and playing with the baby down there. No worries."

No worries.

Stew would try not to worry, but then again, his granddaughter saw nothing wrong with her mother's behavior. It drove Stew nuts. His daughter Emma had such an unnatural obsession with and fears of Yellowstone erupting that her only hobby was preparing for the event. When Cody was three months old, Emma had locked herself in what she called the hole, convinced Yellowstone was going to erupt. It took four deputies and a doctor to get her out of that hole.

In her defense, activity *had* increased in the park, but not enough to cause her to scurry and seal herself in her protective hole.

Medication for a spell and a week away at medical resort got Emma back on track. She still worked on her hobby, but she didn't obsess as much.

At least she didn't do so in front of Stew.

He just wanted a nice, sane family.

Most of them were. He just wished his daughter would stop worrying about the end of the world. One day Stew hoped to get her to see that the chances of civilization ending in her lifetime were slim.

Very slim.

Chapter Two

Ask anyone in town; they'd say that Emma Burton was as crazy as they come.

A nice woman just lacking in reality, as folks would say, odd, and at times, over the top eccentric.

None of that came from her father. Emma's mother nurtured creativity and expressiveness, where Stew was constantly battling Emma to be 'normal'. Emma was, at one time, pretty much normal. She was working for her father when she got pregnant with Heather. There was no college to leave and she didn't have to worry about losing her job. And as close as possible to a shotgun wedding, she married Del before Heather was even born.

Despite the fact that Stew gave them a piece of land and funds to build a home there, Del didn't want to live off of her father, so they lived in an apartment above Bonnie's diner.

Del wanted to take care of his family. Well, that and be a rock star.

He didn't really have a job; he played gigs a lot, but they didn't pay much, and the money to build the house dwindled away, was used to pay bills, get musical equipment for Del and a van for him to haul it.

Emma was supportive. She believed in Del. He was good.

She kept working for her father, except for when she quit and went to work for Mr. Bowman because he paid better at his flannel shirt company.

Of course, Stew wasn't crazy about that and reluctantly matched and beat that extra quarter an hour that Emma was making from Bowman.

Then just about three months before her son, Richie, was due, Del had what he called the opportunity of a lifetime. He went on the road with his band and never came back.

Six months after Richie was born, Del finally called, said he wasn't returning, and he'd do what he could to take care of his family.

That was fifteen years earlier.

She never got in any arguments over child support, because Del didn't pay it. He'd stop by once in a while; the last visit was when Richie turned nine.

Emma kept up with him and his success on the internet and videos.

Emma kept rolling despite it all. She moved in with her parents right away, and her father paid to build her and the kids a house on that piece of land.

But it was during those first few months after Del had left when Emma started searching for a hobby to keep her mind occupied. That's when she discovered information about the super volcano in Yellowstone. From there on, knowing it was fifty thousand years overdue for an eruption, she became obsessed with how she would beat it.

She ended up going to college, night school, studying agriculture. Stew was thrilled. Then he found out her motive was to become an expert in hydroponics.

Which she was.

In a room of the hole, she had a huge hydroponics field set up.

In twelve years, Emma had put over thirty thousand dollars into her 'hole' and other survival extensions to the house. She learned all that she could about what would occur if the eruption took place, and in her mind, she was going to survive.

And so were her children, and now, especially, Cody. She was Emma's primary focus.

She had taken Cody down in the hole to do an inventory of supplies, to see what needed to be rotated. After noticing she'd been down there for several hours, and not wanting to have the police force show up again to haul her out, Emma took the lift up top with her two-year-old granddaughter on her hip.

She sealed up the entrance, using Cody's tiny fingers to turn the lock.

"Good girl. Now, we have to go inside. Gam's gonna see if Uncle Richie will watch you so I can get my hair all cut off."

Cody's hair was wavy and brown, but when the sun hit it, little bits of blonde shown through. She looked a lot like her father, Roman. Despite the fact that her father lived in Hartworth, forty miles away, she actually saw him often.

"Think I'll go short." Emma grabbed Cody's hand and walked with her. "Yeah, short hair will be much easier to keep up in the apocalypse. Don't you think?"

Cody nodded. Not that she knew exactly what she was agreeing to.

Once inside, it was quiet, and Emma spotted Richie on the couch playing a hand held video game. She tapped him on the head to get his attention. When he turned around, Emma signed to him, "Can you watch Cody for a little bit?"

He signed in return, "Where's Heather?"

"She isn't back yet. I have to get my hair cut. I won't be long."

Richie nodded.

"I mean it." Emma gave a stern expression then brought her fingers to her eyes. "Watch her. Do not get distracted."

"Ok." Richie nodded "Ok."

Richie wasn't born deaf. He passed the infant hearing test. And even when he wasn't speaking by two, he passed a second hearing test. It wasn't until he was almost four that they discovered that an undetected ear infection years earlier ruined what he could hear, not the ability to hear. He could hear some, mainly sounds and tones. But they weren't distinguishable. It was once described to Emma by the audiologist that when she spoke to Richie she sounded like Charlie Brown's teacher. Hence why he was speaking like that.

Other than a hearing disability, Richie was a normal teenager. That was why Emma reiterated for him to keep an eye out on Cody. Watch her.

After kissing Cody and Richie, Emma walked to the door. She opened it to find Heather getting ready to enter. "Oh, good, you're home. I was just leaving."

"Where you headed?" Heather asked.

"Hair cut. You know, wanna go short again in case the volcano blows. Easier for me if that happens."

Heather nodded. "Sensible decision."

Emma smiled. "Thanks! I won't be long."

"Oh, Mom." Heather called out as Emma readied to leave. "I accidentally told Pap that you had Cody in the hole. So, stay away from the diner. He's down there people watching."

"Thanks for the heads up, I'll avoid him." And Emma would, or at least would try. She was having a pretty good day, and the last thing she wanted was to deal with an interrogation from her father who seemed to think every time she worked on her project, she had to be institutionalized.

Really that was only once, and Emma was smart enough to know she couldn't let that happen again.

<><><><>

Roman smiled when he opened the message from Heather and saw the picture of his daughter Cody. His phone was full of pictures, and it wasn't as if he didn't see Cody; he did, all the time, even though she was a good distance away. He would have preferred to live in the same town as Heather and Cody, but it wasn't feasible. He grew up in Lincoln, and when the Hartworth town doctor passed away three years earlier, Roman moved there with his father. His father became the new town doctor. His father was all he had, his only family. Roman's mother passed away when he was young. Any other relatives didn't live in America.

At the time of the move, Heather was pregnant and Roman worked for his father at the clinic. He had to keep his job. It was a means of support of his daughter; plus, he and Heather had no plans of marrying or even breaking up. Their relationship was fine with the distance between them. She didn't want to leave her mom. Roman understood that. Heather's mother wasn't always the sanest of human beings.

Emma and Roman's father, Val, didn't get along. Not at all. Emma never trusted his father, and Val believed Emma judged him on the fact that he was an immigrant to America and that she was prejudiced.

They went back and forth all the time. So keeping peace between Heather and Roman entailed keeping distance between Emma and Val.

Another picture came through, and as Roman chuckled at it, he heard a 'thump' in the basement of the clinic. The clinic was the first floor of a big old house, and Roman and his father lived above it.

Roman set down his phone on the counter. He was the only one in the clinic; there were a few emergency appointments in the morning, but he was mainly manning the phones.

He walked to the basement door and hollered down. "Dad, that you?"

"Yes. Yes, it is." His father spoke with a Russian accent.

Roman descended the steps. He stopped near the bottom when he saw the boxes; the oddest were two old big, metal trunks. His father, not a young man, was half bent over, catching his breath. "What's all this?"

"Oh." Val waved out his hand. "The storage facility I have been using for twenty years has closed and I just viewed the notice two days ago. I should check my post office box more frequently."

"Why not get another?"

"I will. I will. But for now, for a few weeks, these will be fine here." Val dusted off his hands and walked to the stairs.

"What is it? I never saw this stuff."

"Some things I brought from Russia, no concern. Just things."

Roman paused in walking up the steps. "Anything cool in there that I can see?"

"Nothing. Just ... just junk." Val looked over his shoulder at the items, reached up, and pulled the string on the light.

Chapter Three

Lincoln, Montana

November 28th

She was beautiful, and Andy watched her walk into the beauty shop on Main Street. How long had he carried a torch for Emma Burton, since the eighth grade, maybe?

Andy was pretty certain that no matter what she did, Emma would always look beautiful. It wasn't a creeper or stalker type of 'torch'; they were friends. They often went to see movies together or had a drink. Andy worked for her father as well as for the town. But even though Emma was basically single for a decade, he never got the nerve to ask her for a real date.

Several factors played into that. He was afraid she'd say no. After all, Andy was viewed as the town idiot because of the way he talked. He wasn't an idiot, not at all. He knew what he wanted to say, he heard it in his mind, but as it came from his head to his mouth, somehow it got lost, and he stuttered. Some times horribly. It was so frustrating for him that he wanted to hit his head to maybe jar it, but then he'd look even more dopey.

He heard people talk as if he didn't understand what they were saying. When they made fun of him calling him a 'retard' or Lenny from *Of Mice and Men*, Andy was still polite, despite how many times he wanted to haul off and deck someone and say, "Heck with you, I'm not an idiot.' But he knew darn well that his mouth would stumble on the 'H' and it would make matters worse. So, he just smiled and nodded.

He related to Emma more than she realized; maybe she did, and that was why she'd go to the movies or shoot pool with him, because she related. They were both viewed as fools. Him for intelligence, her for behavior.

She wasn't any crazier than he was an idiot. It was just the way people perceived them.

Then again, Emma had this thing with him. Unlike others who nodded and waited for him to stutter through his sentence, Emma finished his sentences for him, often calling him funny, witty, or insightful, and believing she knew what he meant because they had a connection. More often than not, she wasn't just wrong, she was way off base.

Like the time he was pruning Mr. Bellow's tree away from the lines. While he was on the ladder, he spotted Mr. Bellow's missing cat on the neighbors back porch roof. But that wasn't the story that Emma walked away with.

"I got .. I got a c … c … cool st st …"

"Story?" Emma said. "You have a cool story to tell? Sweet. I can use a smile, go on."

"I was trim … trim …trimming Mr. Bellows' tr … tr …"

"You were trimming Mr. Bellows' tree?" She questioned and Andy nodded. "Oh, you were on a ladder weren't you?"

Andy nodded.

"This is gonna be good, what did you see?"

"Mr. … B …"

"You saw Mr. Bellows in his window?" Emma shrieked. "Oh my God, was he naked?"

Andy tried to shake his head, but he was so used to nodding, he nodded first. The he finally shook his head, held up his hand, and tried to say he didn't see him naked, but all he got out was, "D …"

"He was in a dress?" Emma laughed loudly. "I knew it. He is so homophobic, that's because he's a cross dresser. This is so good. Did he know you saw him? He did, didn't he? What did you say?"

In his mind, Andy said, "Please let me tell the story," but when the 'P' for please came out, Emma jumped on it.

"You said he was pretty. Oh, God, Andy, you are so funny. Bet he avoids you forever, that is such a funny story, and it'll be our secret."

Andy just smiled. It was a better story than the cat, and who cared if Emma thought Mr. Bellows was a cross dresser.

If anyone else did that to him, Andy would have been frustrated and insulted, but not Emma. He supposed it was his way of keeping her his friend.

He was making his way back up toward the diner when Emma came from the hair place. Her hair was a lot shorter, and it looked really good. He wanted to tell her that and waved as he made his way back down the ladder. She stopped and waited for him to come down.

"Hey, Andy!"

Andy waved.

"You seen my dad? I want to avoid him."

Andy pointed in the diner.

"Jeez, still? It's been hours. Thanks."

"W ... wait." Andy held up a finger then reached out and touched her hair. "B .... Be ... nice." Then he gave a double thumbs up.

"You really think?" Emma played with the ends of her hair that came just to below her collar. "I wanted to go shorter, but she wouldn't cut it shorter. Said I'd get shell-shocked or something. Uh, hello, the apocalypse is gonna take my mind off of that. Now it's gonna get caught in the collar and I'll be flipping it out. But it looks good."

"Aw ... Awesome."

"Aw," she reached up and patted his cheek. "You're so sweet."

Andy cleared his throat.

"What?" Emma asked.

"What the hell did you do to all your hair?" Stew walked up behind her. "If you're gonna cut it short, then go short. Not bobbing along."

Emma gasped. "That's so wrong."

"And so is taking that baby in the hole."

"I did no such thing." Emma folded her arms.

"You're lying," Stew said. "I heard about it."

"Whoever told you that is lying."

"Your daughter told me that."

"There you have it." Emma held out her hand. "She's a liar."

Stew grimaced and then all expression fell from his face. "You gotta be shitting me."

Andy looked and winced.

"What?" Emma asked.

Andy tried to say, "D … De …"

"There's a deer?" Emma asked. "Where?"

Andy shook his head.

"Walk … w … "

"Walk away," Emma nodded. "Oh, good advice. Walk away from my dad."

Stew snapped. "What the hell is the matter with you? Quit putting words in this man's mouth and turn around."

Andy got the word out at the same time Emma turned and looked over her shoulder.

"Del," Andy said.

Del's car was parked a little down the street, and he stepped out with a wave. He was thin, his hair a little longer and blonde. He grinned a wide, perfect smile that could be seen even at a distance.

"Wow, he's still hot," Emma whispered.

Stew nudged her in the arm. "He is not. Please. And he's too old for his hair to be longer than yours."

Del picked up his pace and trotted to her. "Em." With one arm extended, he reached out, wrapped it around her, and embraced her like an old friend.

"Hey … uh, Del." Emma reluctantly returned the embrace.

"Wow, I saw you when I was coming down the street," Del said. "I had to stop before I went to the house." He turned to Stew. "Hey, Dad."

"Um, haven't seen ya in nearly a decade, you lost that right." Stew said. "Stew will work."

Del smiled as if he took it in stride. "And Andy, wow, you look good. Good to see you." He extended his hand.

"D .. Del."

"Still have the stutter, I see."

Emma's mouth dropped open. "You are such an asshole."

Del waved out his hand. "He don't know."

"He does too. And I didn't know you were coming," Emma said.

"Wanted it to be a surprise. I got this great toy dinosaur; I got for Richie, mind if I give it to him before Christmas?" Del asked.

"He's fifteen now," Emma said. "I don't know if he'll play with it. Your granddaughter might."

Del cocked back. "I have a granddaughter? Holy shit. I didn't know that."

Stew interjected. "You might if you called once a year. Are you passing through?"

"No, actually, my tour is on break until after Christmas, so I'm in town," Del said. "Can I stay at the house, Em?"

"No, that won't be a good idea," Emma answered.

"Why not?" Del asked.

"Because it would totally interfere with my … with my …"

Stew finished the sentence. "Not good for a relationship to have an ex-husband staying at the house."

Del laughed. "Yeah, right, I know you, Em. Who can deal with your eccentricities?"

"As a matter of fact … Andy." Emma backed into Andy. "We've been together for a while. We are quite the couple."

"Oh, that makes sense." Del smirked.

Emma spun to Andy. "Can you just deck him? You are much bigger."

Andy shook his head and smiled. "F … f .. it's fine."

Another laugh and Del backed up. "Ok, well, I'm gonna swing by the house, then go and stay with Bill. But, uh, I'll be back tonight. We can hang out."

"I won't be there," Emma said. "Andy and I go out on Fridays. Big date night."

"Then I'll hang with the kids and get to know my granddaughter." Del turned, walked a few steps and then stopped. "Oh, before I go. Does ... uh, Richie still do sign language?"

"Yes, Del, your son is still deaf."

"Just checking." Another turn and Del walked to his car.

Stew grumbled. "What an asshole. And we gotta deal with him for almost a month. I'll kill him before that."

"Thank you, I'd appreciate that," Emma said.

"I gotta go." Stew looked at his watch. "And you have that big date tonight, so do something with that hair." He pointed, kissed his daughter on the cheek, and after shaking hands with Andy, walked away.

With a humbled look, Emma faced Andy. "I'm sorry. It just slipped out that we're dating. It's not all that much of a lie, we do go out once in a while, right?"

Andy nodded. "Yep."

"Do you wanna go out tonight?" Emma asked.

"De … De …" Andy tilted his head.

"A date, yes. Good." Emma tiptoed up and kissed him on the cheek. "Bout time you asked me out officially." She started to go then stopped. "And my hair will look better, I promise."

Emma walked away. She didn't see the huge smile that stayed on Andy's face as she left him.

FLASH FORWARD

Ground Zero – 2

December 23rd

Hartworth, Montana

Edward had been in town only a few hours but already felt as if he had been there for days. Not that he had done all that much work, but he kept thinking about it all.

While he prepared the lab to test the first sample, his team was out and about. They were to count bodies, canvas for survivors, and then collect bodies.

The location of the town worked in their favor; they could hold the news of the town's demise from the media. But for how long? Surely the people in Hartworth knew others outside. It was Christmas, and that told Edward he had two days before he had to release something about Hartworth.

Family and friends would wonder what became of their loved ones on the holiday.

He would have to provide answers.

It saddened him and it scared him.

The cold front that had moved in caused snow and isolation. A combination of wind mixed with the continuous Christmas music caused it to be just too scary. It very well could be a glimpse of the extinction of mankind if they didn't discover what wiped out Hartworth, Montana.

Everything was so gray.

A text message from his wife made him think of his children and how in two days they would scurry about the house jumping for joy over Santa's recent visit. And then he thought of the children of Hartworth who wouldn't get to see Christmas, whose presents were probably tucked away and hidden, while their parents anxiously awaited putting them out.

A Christmas that would never happen.

In the midst of prepping the lab to search for answers, analyze samples, his phone rang.

Edward took the call and accepted the information. Little did he know how vital that information would end up being.

The Centers for Disease Control were calling to tell him that the last phone call was placed three days earlier, and it was one call. Before that it was two whole days. One call to a small town forty miles away called Lincoln.

Edward wrote down the caller's name and address. He would seek out the person, dead or alive, and hopefully find answers. He didn't want to send a team to Lincoln, not yet, but he would have to soon. They needed to find out if someone from Lincoln had been in Hartworth or knew of the virus.

The phone call was brief, but while he was on the phone he heard two assistants enter in the back. He knew why they had returned.

They were bringing Edward a body to examine to get a sample and to start learning about the virus.

After ending the call, Edward was ready to suit up again. A glass wall separated him from the lab and another window from the autopsy room. He signaled that he would be right there. One of his assistants, Harold Daily, waved his arm and indicated to Edward to pick up the interoffice phone.

Edward did. "What's up, Harold?" he asked.

Harold spoke through the radio system in his suit. "We saw some weird shit out there."

"So weird that you couldn't wait until I came in there?" Edward asked.

"Actually yeah. Megan and I have to prep the body. While she starts, I'm gonna upload the photos I took. The body needs to warm up some."

Edward nodded. "Upload them." He hung up the phone, walked to the coffee pot and poured a cup of coffee, then made his way to the computer.

He lifted the phone once more. "They uploaded?"

"Yeah," Harold answered.

Edward clicked on the folder. The first picture was of the young man in the pickup truck holding the shotgun. "What am I looking at?"

"The first house."

Edward clicked the picture. "Ok. What about it."

"Empty." Harold said. "Next house, empty. We hit about fifteen houses in the main portion of town. All empty. Population 843 and the first batch of houses was empty."

"Did they leave? Oh, God. .."

"Wait. Click the fire station."

Edward stared at a picture of the building's exterior. "What about it."

"The sign on the door." Harold explained. "It reads ..."

The next photo zoomed in.

"Stay out. Infected!" Harold recited. "And then we went inside."

Edward's stomach dropped when he looked at the first picture. Inside the fire station were hundred of bodies. People were lying on blankets and sleeping bags. It appeared they tried to set up a medical area.

"And this is one of three we found so far," Harold stated. "We're going to keep checking houses, but my guess is we'll find more spots like this. Dead men in pickup trucks with guns were placed on all access roads in and out of this town."

Edward sat back, took a deep breath, and rubbed his chin. "So basically they shut the town down and quarantined themselves."

"Yes," Harold said. "Looks that way. Something horrific ravished this town quickly, but not so quick that they couldn't take time to set up medical aid stations."

"They knew it was coming," Edward stated.

"That's my guess."

"Wow." Although not a medical word, it was the best Edward could muster. "Wow. They knew it was coming. Locked down tight to keep it in. Yet they didn't tell a soul…" Edward's eyes shifted to the information he received from the CDC regarding the last phone call. "Or did they?"

Chapter Four

Lincoln, Montana

November 28th

His father was an idiot.

That was what Richie thought as he kicked back on the couch replying to his father via text message. He didn't mean to disrespect the man who was a vital part of his creation, but his father was clueless. How he acquired any kind of fame was beyond Richie. He played guitar well and sang even better, but somewhere people had to notice he wasn't bright.

He sent the word, 'sure' in reply to the question, 'Can we text?"

The texting question wasn't about communicating on a regular basis, it was a request for when his father stopped by. Del stated he didn't know the sign language thing.

It cracked Richie up to think his father was so naïve that he could stumble into town nearly a decade later and all would be fine. Richie wouldn't be mean, not at all, but he certainly didn't hold a candle for his father. Heather did, for some odd reason.

"Daddy is famous," she'd say.

Yeah, well, Dad's been on the cover of every tabloid for cheating on his last two wives.

Heather didn't notice.

Richie didn't want to text anymore. He wanted to get back to his word game, so he sent his father a message that he'd see him when he got there and returned to his game. No sooner had he done that, his mother's hand laid upon his shoulder and when she drew his attention, she signed, "Can you get the door? My hair isn't done."

"Ok," Richie signed. "Who is it?"

"Andy."

Richie nodded and got off the couch while his mother scurried away and up the stairs. He opened the door.

Andy smiled as Richie opened the door wider.

"Come in," Richie signed. "My mother is doing her hair. She'll be right down."

A nod and Andy closed the door.

"So you guys are hanging tonight?" Richie asked.

That was when Andy returned the signing and did so smoothly. "Actually, we have a date."

"No way."

"Yes, your mother asked me out."

"Cool. It's about time."

"I agree." Andy raised his eyes when he heard footsteps on the stairs, and Emma raced into the room.

"I'm ready," she said and signed.

Andy spoke, "D … did … y … you … hungry?"

"Oh, yeah, I can eat. I'm starved. I'm in the mood for ribs. They have the rib special at Bronco's tonight. Unless you don't like ribs."

Andy shook his head. "No that … s … sow …s."

"Salmon, you want salmon? Hmm." Emma scratched her head. "We may have to go outside the county for good salmon, but I'll put it in your hands. Surprise me."

Andy chucked. "K … K … ok. Hey …" He reached out. "Pur … pur …"

"My purse. Thank you." Emma spun and hurried away.

Richie who had witnessed it and was pretty good at reading lips, tapped Andy's arm for attention. "Does she interrupt everything you say?"

"She always does," Andy signed. "She tries to guess what I am saying, so I don't have to struggle. She guessed wrong."

Richie laughed. "Oh my God, that's so funny yet so wrong."

Andy shrugged.

"You should just sign."

"No, she doesn't know I sign, and it's more entertaining this way."

"Ready," Emma announced, entering the room. "Oh, look, you were signing. I didn't know you signed."

Andy held his fingers an inch apart.

"A little is better than none," Emma said. "I'll teach you. Especially if we make this a regular thing, this dating. Wait. Too forward?"

Andy shook his head.

"Good." Emma leaned over and kissed Richie. "Feel free to lock the door, not answer, or even call the cops when your dad shows up."

"I'll be fine," Richie replied. "Have fun."

"Don't wait up," Emma said as she walked to the door and paused, looking at Andy. "Wait. Was that forward."

Andy held up his fingers again to signify 'a little,' and then with a smile, he opened the door.

◇◇◇◇

They really had a date?

They called it that?

Did they say where they're going?

Thanks.

Stew got the information he wanted; he was curious, because he saw Andy drive through town in a clean pickup truck and combed hair.

So he called his grandson, Richie.

Richie gave him all the information he needed, and Stew, just to be 'that kind of guy', went to Broncos to watch his daughter.

Not to make her nervous or embarrass her, but to make sure she didn't screw up. The last thing he wanted was for Emma to be alone. She hadn't dated in years. She went to have drinks with Andy often, but it was never a date.

Stew knew Andy was a good guy.

He also knew Andy was the only man in town or in the state of Montana that could deal with Emma.

His daughter needed that, and Stew needed someone to keep her in line.

Andy had the potential to pull her from her insane world into a semi-insane world, because Emma would never be normal.

Dinner was excellent, and Emma wasn't really surprised that conversation didn't fly; she didn't expect it to with Andy. Typically, they just met for drinks, played pool or darts, and talked very little. But it was a pseudo date and Emma was making the best of it, especially since not only was Andy paying, he decided on ribs for her when he was in the mood for salmon.

Since he was communicating with Richie, Emma decided to teach him some sign language over dinner. Andy picked it up pretty quickly; she felt guilty about one thing she taught him. Eventually she would tell him that when he thought he was signing, 'are you having a good time?' he was actually saying, "You're the coolest chick I know."

Emma snickered at that, but Andy kept signing it and grasped it like a pro.

There was something different about the night. Andy looked different. It wasn't just the hair cut he got for the occasion. Emma couldn't place her finger on it.

They headed to the Tilt and Twist, an earthy bar just on the outskirts of Lincoln. It was pretty busy, but it was Friday, the closet bar to town, and karaoke night. She wasn't surprised to see her father at the bar when she walked in. Of course, he would be there, spying. Stew merely waved, lifted a drink, and commented that her hair looked better and that she should have worn something other than jeans.

She dragged Andy from the handshake to grab a pool table while one was open. Andy quickly placed down a few games worth of quarters.

"You're so on," Emma told Andy. "And I am not taking it easy on you because it's date night." She chalked up her stick.

He found the one he would use, looked at Emma and signed. "You're the coolest chick I know."

Emma laughed. "I am having a great time, thanks." She paused and lowered her head. "Can I tell you something?"

Andy nodded.

Emma walked to him. "You're the coolest guy I know."

Andy laughed with a throw back of his head.

"I'm serious. Don't make fun of me. Why are you laughing?"

Andy shook his head. "Not … not used to c …. c …"

"Compliments?"

He gave a thumbs up.

"You should be; you are a great guy, Andy. And can I tell you a secret?"

"Y … yes."

"I've kinda always liked you."

Andy moistened his lips, moved closer to Emma, leaned down some and said. "I .. k … k ..kind of …." He struggled with a twitch of his head.

"Have a girlfriend?"

Andy's head cocked.

"I'm sorry."

Andy facially ridiculed.

"What?"

"No. I l … l …."

"Left your wallet in the car?"

"Em …"

"Look at me like a sister?"

"Em …"

"Like us better as friends? I'm going through all the 'L' words here, help me out."

Immediately his hand shot to her mouth and he shook his head. He stepped back, held up a finger, and then signed to her. "No, I kind of have always liked you, too."

Emma's mouth dropped open. "You learn really fast. Holy crap. I never knew anyone to pick up sign language that quickly."

Andy shook his head and signed. "I have known it for years. You of all people should know it's the first thing they teach you in speech therapy. I've been going to therapy since the accident."

"Then if you …" she gasped. "Oh, you dick." She swiped playfully at him. "Then you knew I taught you wrong."

"Yes," Andy said.

Emma laughed. "You are so getting beat tonight for sure." Suddenly the smile dropped from her face.

Andy looked over his shoulder, then back to Emma with a roll of his eyes. "Ig … ignore him. P … play."

Emma growled and racked the balls. "Why is he here? Oh, great, he's coming over. Hey, he doesn't sign, we can talk about him, and he won't know what we're saying."

Andy snapped his finger and pointed to the pool table, then lifted the rack. "B … B .. break."

Emma did. It wasn't a very good break, more than likely because she wasn't concentrating. Especially because she saw Del walk to the pool table.

"I didn't cause that, did I?" Del asked.

"No," Emma answered. "Why are you here?"

"It's the only kicking bar around." Del replied. "And I'm being friendly. I bought you guys a drink. Your next round is on me."

"Wow. Cool. Thanks. Wondered what you did with all that money," Emma said, watching Andy take his turn. She winced when he made his shot and seemingly just played as if Del wasn't there.

"You're getting your ass beat," Del said.

"I see that."

"Em, come on, be nice. I'm gonna be in town for a while."

"Why is that?" Emma spun to him. "We haven't seen you in years."

"I've been busy," Del replied. "Your turn."

Emma grunted. She just knew any shot she took wasn't going to be her best. She lined it up, aimed, revved back, took a shot, and missed.

Del snickered. "Sorry. Hey, I'm not interrupting date night. Andy seems pissed you aren't talking."

"You are interrupting date night," Emma said, "and he's just concentrating."

Andy looked around the table for a shot. "Em," he called then signed what he was going to shoot for.

"Really?" Del asked. "He signs?"

"Yes, so he can communicate with your son," Emma said smugly.

"What did he say?"

"He said he's a big fan of you on YouTube." She shook her head. "None of your business what he said." She watched Andy take a shot.

"Sign language is good. For him. At least," Del said, "he won't stutter that way. Unless he gets a twitch in his hand."

"Oh my God." Emma grunted and spun to Andy. "For the love of all that is good will you please just deck him. Hit him. I won't say a word. Go."

Andy just laughed. He shook his head, kissed Emma on the forehead, and took another shot.

"Cute," Del commented. "Anyhow, I'll let you guys go." He turned, stopped, and looked at Andy. "I'm gonna sing Karaoke tonight. What do you say, Andy?"

Andy gave a thumbs up.

"Good. I'll put you in, too." Del turned.

"Whoa!" Emma hurried to Del. "What the hell is the matter with you?"

"What? I'm gonna put Andy in to sing." Del shrugged. "What's the big deal?"

"He didn't say he would."

"Actually, Em, he didn't say anything." Del choked out a laugh. "This will be interesting." Del waved to Andy. "See …see… see you A … A… A.. Andy."

"Asshole," Emma commented as Del walked away. She returned to Andy. "He's putting your name in."

Andy shrugged. "It's ….so ….so … kay."

"Really? You'll sing?"

Andy nodded. "You … you .. lost."

Emma looked at the empty table. "Shit. I'll rack." She walked to the table. "You don't have to sing."

"So…so… Kay. I sing."

"Oh. You never did before."

Another shrug from Andy.

"Are you any good?"

"I'm okay."

Okay.

Andy said he was 'okay'. Admittedly, Emma was nervous for Andy when he got up to sing. She was. Del had just done a karaoke version of his own song, rocking the house, getting a standing ovation, and then Andy stepped up.

He whispered to the DJ what he wanted to sing and never took the microphone off the stand.

Emma downed a shot.

Her own father stood with her, telling her that, after Andy was done, he was going to personally take Del from the bar.

Emma felt relieved by that. The last thing Andy needed was to be even more humiliated by Del. After all, Del was an awesome singer.

But in actuality, Del couldn't hold a candle to Andy.

The song was slow, but not so much a ballad as an inspirational tune. At the first note, the first word, Emma stumbled back.

There was Andy. Tall, fit, rough around the edges, yet the smooth, tenor voice with emotions just blew her away. An occasional rasp crept in as he sang, but Andy didn't look at the words on the screen, he just sang.

More than anything, Emma wanted to take a picture of Del's reaction. Obviously, Andy was a better singer. Hands down. But she didn't look at Del; she couldn't take her eyes off of Andy.

'Good Lord,' her father whispered beside her. "Is that our Andy singing?"

All she kept saying was 'Oh my God.' It got to the point that she moved closer to the stage and then just sat down. Emma was proud and awestruck. She wanted to scream 'again' and 'more' when he finished. But he wouldn't have heard her through the screams and cheers.

Everyone that knew Andy hadn't a clue that he sung like a pro.

She swore at that moment that any crush she had on Andy magnified, because she just saw a new side.

He didn't need to deck Del physically, because he knocked him out in another way.

When Andy walked toward Emma, she threw her arms around him and shrieked, "That was unbelievable. Holy shit."

"Son," Stew extended a hand. "Who would have known?"

"Th … thanks." Andy nodded. "I … know the DJ from H…Hartworth."

"Will you sing again, please?" Emma asked. "Please, I'll sign you up."

"M .. ma … maybe." He then pointed to the pool table.

Del never bothered them the rest of the night, never said a word about Andy's singing or approached them.

But that wasn't the end of the night even though they left the bar just before midnight.

Andy asked her if she wanted to hang out a bit, he'd make them some food.

When he said, "I saw yours, you now can see mine," Emma thought the wrong way. She had no idea he was talking about houses, until after she told him. "I like you and all, Andy, but there's just some things a girl has to do to herself to be playing-the-field ready. Plus, I'm not wearing bedroom-friendly underwear."

He laughed, like he always did. Andy always laughed, but somehow Emma wasn't seeing a smiling man who didn't know better; she saw a different man who just knew how to take things in stride.

When Andy extended the invitation to Emma, he was hoping he wasn't being too forward. In fact, he worried about that after she made the bedroom-friendly underwear comment. But he conveyed that it was just to hang out. After all, the night felt different. A part of him didn't feel like a creep anymore for having such a crush on her, considering she liked him, too.

His apartment wasn't much, but he had been to Emma's home a thousand times. He worked for her father and he'd go to Emma's under the guise that he was fixing things, when actually he was helping her with something in 'the hole'.

Andy saw no problem with her Yellowstone obsession; it was based in both reality and science. Andy's only concern was that if they were so close, the ventilation pipe could be buried beneath rubble and ash.

Andy fixed that and was impressed with his creation. The ventilation pipe retracted, and the top that 'popped' open was actually close to a drill bit used to drill for oil and pipes, a smaller version. Emma only needed to retract the pipe until the debris had fallen and then drill it to the surface. If nothing was there, she only had to raise the pipe a little bit, but if need be, the pipe extended close to seven feet above the ground. Andy's idea.

But Emma had never been to his place. She was at his house when he lived with his parents, but when they died, Andy sold the house and got the apartment above Bonnie's Diner.

It was a great deal. Bonnie always sent leftover daily specials from the day for Andy instead of throwing them out.

In fact, he had some beef stew. His plan was to make some biscuits, have some stew while watching a movie.

He wasn't thinking about being physical; he was just happy to spend time with Emma. And it was still early.

Emma's comment of 'oh, wow, this is so cute', when she walked in, made Andy smile.

Andy wouldn't call his apartment 'cute' more so basic, small, clean, and plain. The entrance led into the living room which had a dinette area and an open kitchen defined by a counter.

Andy could see Emma in his living room as he pulled items from the fridge.

"Dr . … Drink?" he asked.

"Um, yes, please, anything you have will work." Emma stared at the tall, wall-length bookshelf. "This is amazing, you must like books."

Andy handed her a beer. "Yes."

Her fingers trailed across the spines. "None of these are fiction. They're all …." She stopped. "Wait a second." She pulled a hard back, coffee table-style book from the shelf. "Bog World, by Andrew Jenkins?" She spun to Andy. "Is that you?"

Andy nodded. He didn't think for a second that Emma would look at the names of the books he had.

"You wrote a book?"

Andy held up his hand.

"Five?" Emma gasped. "Are they all about … what the hell is a Bog person?" She flipped through the book. "Oh my God. They're like mummies."

Andy pursed his lips and swallowed and, like singing, he recited the words he had spoken to himself out loud. "They are a form of mummy. Naturally mummified. They are found mainly in Ireland and have quite the story. Most died violent deaths, unlike the Ice Age mummies." He reached for another book and handed it to her.

Emma didn't take it. She just stared. "I'm sorry … you .. you didn't stutter."

"Not … w…. when I ….s …s…talk about things I n …know."

"Holy cow." Emma flipped open the book. "You're an anthropologist? What the heck? Why are you being the town handyman and stable guy when you have a degree in Anthropology and … you write books?"

"I d … d… did for years. Museum. Went … went abroad. It's too d … d… difficult."

"I'm pissed at you, Andy." She looked at the shelf and pulled down another book. "All these years and I asked you what you went to school for and you said digging and studying dead people."

Andy actually told her more than that, but he never used the word anthropology, because it was too difficult to say. "Sorry."

"Here I thought you went to school to be a mortician and grave digger and didn't have it in you to embalm … Jesus." She shook her head. "You need to tell people this. You deserve much more credit than people give you."

"N … nah. I … like when p …p …people think I'm d -dumb. I lis … listen to th … th … them and n … n… know they are the ones who are dumb."

"Did you sell a million copies?"

Andy laughed; he wanted to tell her he was lucky he sold a hundred and barely made his small advance back on the Bog People book. "No."

She spun quickly to him. "I want to buy one. Where can I get one?" Emma asked excitedly.

Andy held up his finger and walked to a closet. He reached to the stop shelf and pulled down a box, carrying it to her and dropping it at her feet.

"Oh, wow," Emmie said. "Look how many. I'll buy them all, thank you."

"W … What? No." Andy laughed. "No."

"Please. This will be my Christmas present to everyone. I was gonna go to Wal-Mart and have a portrait taken in a bad sweater and give it out, but this is much better and cooler."

Andy shook his head.

"Think about it?"

"I …th … th … think about it."

"Cool." She quickly kissed him on the cheek and took a book from the box. "This is so awesome. I am so proud of you, Andy. I am. You write books and sing like you should be on a talent TV show. Plus, you're this really great guy on top of all this." She embraced the book like it was a treasure. "The worst mistake you made was showing me this."

"I … d-didn't show. You … you .. . found it."

"I did. I did." Emma nodded with a smile. "And I'm telling everyone."

Andy exhaled with a shake of his head, and then looked back when the timer went off on the stove. He walked to the kitchen, leaving Emma in the living room.

"Seriously, Andy, this is just the beginning."

Andy looked at her from the kitchen.

"Just the beginning."

And it was. The beginning of a turn in their friendship and the beginning of a new life for Andy. He just didn't know it yet.

FLASH FORWARD

Ground Zero – 3

December 23rd

Hartworth, Montana

Nature had frozen Vivian Morris, and she barely decomposed. She was one of three bodies Edward's team had retrieved from the fire station. There was a whole town outside his lab, a whole town that was dead, and the three bodies were just the start. Before they did accountability, called for reserve units and collected bodies, Edward had to find answers.

Something vicious wiped out the town of Hartworth.

He believed it wouldn't take long to find out what it was.

But the temperatures were cold, and he had to wait until Vivian thawed some.

He knew she had been dead only for a few days. The circumstances of the town told him that, not the frozen body.

While he waited on her to thaw, he learned who she was. She was wearing a paper wrist band, handmade and stapled together. It had her name and age. Someone took care to make sure that when the bodies were discovered, so were their identities.

But Vivian's purse was next to her; in it was her bi-fold. The thirty-seven-year-old woman appeared to have two children and a husband. There was a dated wallet size photo of her and her family.

It wasn't taken long ago. Her children were young.

Edward thought of his own children, and sadness hit him He had to dismiss it quickly. For the time being, anyway.

Vivian was beautiful in the picture, nothing like the desiccated corpse before him. She was, like the other bodies, black.

It reminded him of pictures of Bog People he saw, completely black, mouths open, screaming in pain, frozen in the last moment of death.

It appeared as if she were missing a lot of her skin, like a burn victim. But she wasn't burnt. Her body was so dark it masked any hypo stasis that could be present.

As she became workable, he lifted her eyelids. The sclera and gums were black, as well; there was no pink on her body.

Edward hated even the thought of cutting her open, but he had to.

Taking a blood sample from her was difficult; he chalked it up to the blood still being cold. He was able to retrieve some, enough to view in a microscope, but it, like Vivian, was black.

He began audibly speaking his autopsy. "Not much epithelia remains on the body …" he sliced into her forearm, lifting a section of skin. He choked on a gag when he lifted it and everything underneath pulled like a gluey dark substance.

But that wasn't the worst. That was when Edward dove into her torso, needing only to make a single lateral incision across her abdomen to know he was dealing with something new.

Edward had to stop, just for a little bit. A moment to catch his bearings after seeing her internal organs.

It was frightening. In all his years, he had never encountered anything like it.

Whatever struck Hartworth did it so fast and to such an unusual extent, that they told no one and the town was wiped out.

Someone in town knew what it was. Someone in town knew it was coming enough to set up an aid station.

Time frame.

It was December 23rd. The last call out of the town was a single call placed on December 20th. Before that, nothing for two days. Vivian more than likely died on December 21st.

Was the last call for help, to say good bye?

With the lack of communication out of Hartworth between the 18th and 20th, that told Edward the town was sick and dying,

Everything was normal, phone communications, bank transactions, all normal until the 18th.

The first ones probably started getting sick on December 17th.

To set up an aid station took knowledge that it was coming and of an extremely fast incubation period. Fast enough to perch a guard on every access road. Why did they keep it a secret?

Allowing a one-to-two-day incubation period, combined with the fact that someone had knowledge of the bug, Edward pinpointed his ground zero day.

The day it all started. But what caused it? Was it released? Was there an accidental experiment?

Edward would solve this mystery. He was bound and determined to find out what happened out of the ordinary in Hartworth, Montana, on December 16th.

Chapter Five

Hartworth, Montana

December 16th

"Thank you, Vivian, thank you so much." Roman was excited and rightfully so. Everything was falling into place, and Vivian Morris was the final piece he needed to put it together. Three employees other than him worked for his father. Vivian was the only person available to cover for him.

Enthusiastically he sent a text to Heather, his fingers fumbling and making spelling errors. He couldn't help it. They both wanted to see the concert in Billings but couldn't afford tickets when they went on sale. When they had the money, the concert was sold out, all 22,000 seats. The concert was huge, three bands. So when he won those tickets from the radio station, Roman was through the roof. He had tried six times a day, day and night, for a week to win them. Problem was, he just won them, and the concert was that night.

But he needed his shift covered for the evening and for the next morning, because he and Heather would stay overnight in Billings. Vivian Morris pulled through.

Heather's mom would watch the baby, another dilemma solved.

His father was fine … sort of … with him going, he just had to make sure all the work was done and ready for the morning.

Roman set down his phone, grabbed a tablet, and started making a list. The clinic door opened and he looked down to his watch as he stood behind the reception window.

"Hey, Mr. Rudolph, you're a little early." Roman said.

"I know. I know. The wife had to shop." The older gentleman said as he hung up his coat. "I'll wait."

"No problem. Relax." Roman had all the charts pulled for the day. He grabbed Mr. Rudolph's and tucked it under his arm as he walked to the back. He placed the chart in the basket of exam room one and headed to his father's office.

"Dad," Roman knocked on the door and opened it. The room was empty. "Where the heck did he go?" The clinic wasn't that big. He headed back down the hall. That was when he noticed the basement door was ajar. He opened it slightly and called down the steps. "Dad? You down here?"

"Yes, Roman, I am."

He took a few steps downward. "What are you doing down here again?"

"The temperature has dropped," Val replied. "I am just checking my storage things. I will be moving them after the holiday."

"Really?" Roman reached the bottom of the stairs and his father stood before a trunk. It was closed. "I thought you said this was just all old junk."

Val nodded.

"Why are you worried?" Roman asked.

"Because it is junk that has been with me for years. Just because I called it junk does not mean I want it to be ruined."

"Ah, okay. Mr. Rudolph is here."

"Fine. Thank you. Please leave."

Roman cocked back some at the harsh dictate of his father. After a shrug, he walked up the stairs. He looked back as he reached the top and closed the door.

Odd. He found his father's behavior odd. It was the third time in a week his father had gone down to the basement to check on those items.

For something so worthless, his father was acting as if he held a priceless secret down there. But to Roman, it couldn't be all that important if it was just stuck in a basement.

◇◇◇◇

Lincoln, Montana

Like he did every morning, Stew perched himself in his favorite booth at Bonnie's diner. He was already on his second cup of coffee after dropping Richie off at school.

He called Heather, asked her to join him; she said she'd be right down. That was forty minutes earlier. Stew would wait.

His work was done for the day, having started before dawn.

Besides, he'd wait for Heather. He adored his granddaughter. He loved Richie, but Heather always held that special spot with him.

He watched her walk in, brush the snowflakes from her head; she wasn't wearing a heavy coat and that irritated Stew.

"Sorry for taking so long, Pap."

"Where's your coat?" he asked. "You're gonna get sick."

"I'm fine." She waved him off. "It's not that cold. Just snowy. Did you hear me?"

"I don't pay attention when you or your mother is late. That's who I was with."

"She wasn't in the hole, was she?"

"Nope. Not … you know ... yet."

Stew grumbled.

"She did say seismic activity was up for Yellowstone. It's based in reality."

"I agree," Stew said, "but not reality in her lifetime. Is she gonna watch the baby?"

"Oh, yeah, that isn't the problem. The problem came when I asked."

"What do you mean?"

"Well, I made the mistake of saying Roman's father offered."

Stew exhaled. "Why would you do that? You know she hates him."

"I know. I still think Mom's the reason he took the job in Hartworth."

"Well, she picketed the man's home, for Christ's sake. Even I called the cops on her."

Heather laughed and looked up when Bonnie approached. "Morning, Bonnie."

"Hey, Heather, does doc still have evening hours tonight?"

"Late hours, till six. What's up? You sick?" Heather asked.

"No." Bonnie poured her a coffee. "My knee is overdue for a shot of cortisone. Was hoping to squeeze in sometime after four."

"Hold on," Heather pulled out her phone and her fingers flew as she punched in letters.

"Couldn't you call?" Stew asked.

"Easier this way. Val hates when the phone rings." Heather's phone beeped and she looked. "Five thirty good?" she asked Bonnie.

"Perfect, thank you. Extra order of bacon on me." She winked and walked off.

"I didn't order." Heather said to Stew.

"It's breakfast, you don't need to."

"Ok," she shrugged. "Hey, is that my dad in the corner booth."

"Yep." Stew didn't turn around.

"He's up early. Is that the Gray Grocer checkout lady from Hartworth?"

"Yep."

"Hmm. He dates the strangest women."

"Heather," Stew snapped. "You aren't that naïve, are you?"

"What do you mean?"

"Never mind." Stew shook his head. "So you have this concert."

"Oh it's gonna be so great, Pap. The Yards, Don Simmons, and Ace of Hearts."

Stew nearly choked. "My God, those bands are from decades ago, those people gotta be my age."

Heather nodded.

"Who the hell wants to see old rockers?"

"It's not age, Pap, it's music, and it's good. And … my dad is leaving …" Her head turned as Del walked right by her. "Maybe he didn't see me."

"I'm sure," Stew said. "Now let's talk about this concert."

And they did, Heather called it life changing and that the night was gonna be like no other. Little did she know how right she was.

◇◇◇◇

Cody's fingers were tiny, and Emma was amazed how she moved them and controlled them with ease. Although her little droplet of icing on the cookies for a face were a little skewed, Emma was proud.

"Good. Good girl. Ain't that good, Andy?" She looked up to Andy who was working on his own cookie creation.

"G … great."

Emma smiled. "Andy's jealous. Man of little words, that's how you can tell he's jealous," Emma told the little one. "But it's nice of him to come over and play today."

"Yes, Gam. It is," Cody said with excitement. She tucked her growing hair behind her ears, smoothing it from her face. She took her task at hand very seriously.

"Maybe with Gam being in charge tonight," Emma said, "Andy can come over and play tonight?" She winked.

Andy shook his head. "B … busy. S .. sorry." He then laughed.

"Asshole," Emma said then turned to Cody. "Andy is joking. He'll be by tonight. We'll get pizza."

"Pizza?" Cody asked.

"Yes and we'll …" Emma stopped talking when the alarm on her phone beeped in a siren style mode. She grabbed it. "Oh, God. Yellowstone erupted." She jumped up and swooped the baby into her arms. "We gotta get to the hole. We have four minutes."

"Run, Gam, run," Cody said.

Emma raced toward the front door and Andy stopped her before she ran out. "Andy, what? The ventilation pipes need checked before we go down there."

"I …" Andy nodded his words. "G … got. Go. Re-retract from b … below."

With shivering breath, Emma nodded. "Hurry. You don't have much time. The cloud is on its way and it will sweep you away."

When she said that, Cody screamed.

"It's ok, baby, we're gonna be okay." Emma, cradling the child, raced back to the kitchen. She opened the basement door, pulled it closed behind her and ran down the steps.

She ran across the unfinished basement to the laundry room and to the tall white cabinet next to the washing machine under the single well window. It wasn't a cabinet at all. When opened it exposed a metal door.

Emma quickly punched in her code. The door slid to the right and she went inside. With the baby she raced down a twenty-foot hall until she arrived at another door. That one was open. She ran inside, sealed the door, and set down the baby.

The room resembled a family room. "Stay here, Cody. Play with the toys."

Cody nodded, and Emma ran into another hall. She arrived to see the ventilation system already on its way into the shelter. Andy had beaten her to the punch by manually lowering it.

"Come on, Andy,"

She looked up and down the halls and didn't see him. She had to worry about Cody, so she returned to the family-style room to hold her granddaughter.

She waited.

One minute, two.

Surely the cloud passed. But no Andy.

After ten minutes, Emma knew he wasn't arriving.

"I guess it's just you and me," Emma told Cody. "Thank God, I have you, baby. Thank God." She kissed the child. "Maybe Andy came in one of the other entrances. What do you think?"

Cody nodded; she didn't seem scared at all.

"Let's go check."

The 'hole' was huge. It was actually as big as Emma's ranch home, but built underground. A family-style room, a kitchen and eating area, two sleeping rooms, showers and toilets. The hydroponic room and the storage facility, which held the tank of water, were bigger than the other rooms combined.

There were two other entrances into the 'hole' other than the house.

One was a door in the storage area. It led down a small tunnel to a hidden hatch in a nearby storage barn. The other was located at the far end of the shelter, another tunnel that went to the yard. It was a steel tube, much like the ones in the bunkers of the eighties.

But Andy was nowhere to be seen.

Emma gave Cody some cookies and placed her in front of a cartoon. After about twenty minutes, the child grew restless and Emma grew irritated.

"What the hell, right?" She asked Cody.

"Right."

"It's been close to a half hour. Jeez. Let's find him." Emma sighed out, grabbed Cody and left the shelter. She secured it again behind her and they emerged back into the basement.

She heard footsteps above her head, and she walked back to the kitchen, holding the baby.

"Andy," she called out as she opened the door. "What the heck. This was a drill. Yellowstone erupted. You died." Her final words trailed as she saw Andy cringe and then noticed her father standing there. "Shit."

Stew folded his arms and looked at Andy. "So you're encouraging this?"

Andy lifted his hands.

"You know, Daddy," Emma said. "He is encouraging because he's smart. He knows why civilizations didn't survive when they should have. The Bog People. Ice Age Eskimos. All died in the middle of doing something because they weren't prepared enough. That won't be me."

"Uh, huh." Stew nodded. "You aren't an Ice Age Eskimo. Or a Bog Person."

"I certainly hope not," Emma said. "I have no plans of dying in an extinction level event."

"You're a nut," Stew said.

Andy laughed.

"Oh, you think that's funny?" Emma asked. "No sleep over tonight, pal."

"Emma," Stew scolded. "This behavior with Cody …"

"Will save her life one day," Emma cut him off. "So there."

"Maybe you should have let Val watch …"

Emma's loud gasp silenced Stew. "Bite your tongue." She gave a quick look to Andy. "Did you hear that? He wants the spy to watch my granddaughter. Uh … no, Daddy. I don't even like when she visits him. He speaks Russian to her. Lord knows what vile things he is saying."

"Um, Em?" Stew said, "The Cold War ended. Val is a doctor, not a Russian spy, and you need to stop this."

"I hate him." Emma folded her arms. "I hate him, Andy, and he hates me."

"He does not," Stew defended.

"Daddy, he was the one who had me committed."

Stew growled, "Because you wouldn't come out of the goddamn hole!"

"I thought the world was gonna end!" Emma yelled. "And he used it as his excuse to get me away because he knew I found his picture on the 'net." She faced Andy. "I found his picture on the internet. He's a missing spy. I'll show you."

Stew tossed his hands in the air. "Let it go, for crying out loud. You are both grandparents to that child."

"I don't trust him."

With another growl, Stew turned. "I'm leaving."

"Why are you here?" Emma asked.

"I don't know now. I forgot. You frustrate me. I'll be back." Stew walked out the back door.

Emma chuckled. "And he calls me crazy."

Andy laid a hand on her cheek. "You … you're fine."

"Thank you." She tiptoed up and darted a kiss to Andy.

"I … want … t… to see …"

"The spy picture of Val?"

Andy nodded.

"Absolutely. But first …" She placed Cody back at the table, pulled the cookie decorations to her and then grabbed her phone, resetting it. "We will do the drill again. Right this time."

◇◇◇◇

Hartworth, Montana

Val kissed Heather on the cheek as he placed on his coat. "I will be making rounds at the hospital so I will not get to see you two off."

"Thank you," Heather said. "For letting Roman get time off."

"Have fun." He stepped to Roman and kissed him on the forehead. "Drive safely and call when you arrive."

"We will, Father. Thanks."

Val grabbed his briefcase and walked from the clinic, waving one more time.

Heather spun to Roman. "All right, what's left to do?"

"I did all the work, we can leave as soon as Vivian gets here."

"Sweet."

"Hey …" Roman leaned to her. "We got about fifteen minutes. No patients. Wanna do something we're not supposed to?"

"Fool around?" Heather asked.

"No." Roman grabbed her hand. "The basement."

"Seriously?" Heather asked. "You mean the stuff that your father is obsessed with?"

"Yeah, aren't you curious as to what it is?" Roman asked.

"You bet." Heather looked at her phone. "Ok, let's look, but we don't have much time. We don't want Vivian to bust us down there and tell your dad."

"Cool, let's go."

Roman led the way to the basement, leaving the door open. He turned on the light. Setting center were several boxes and two old trunks.

"Why do you suppose he is obsessive about this?" Heather asked.

"I'm betting there are pictures in here. He doesn't talk about living in Russia at all."

"Was he a doctor there?" Heather asked.

"Yeah. He was a lot older than my mother." Roman began going through the boxes. The flaps weren't sealed. "Books."

Heather checked another box. "Oh my God."

"What?"

"How freaking old are these boxes?" She lifted a tape from one. "These aren't even VHS; they're the ones before it."

"Oh wow. Beta?" Roman laughed and took the tape. "This is so great."

"Let's try the trunks." Heather walked to the first trunk. They both knelt on the floor.

"It can't be all that secretive," Roman said as he turned the key. "He left the key in the lock." As he opened the trunk lid, the key fell out. He didn't think much of it, he'd get it later.

Inside the trunk were books, some clothes, and a few pictures.

Heather's hands rummaged at the same time as Roman's. "What's in here that he's so protective over?"

"I don't know. Maybe there's a diary or an old girlfriend."

"Oh, maybe he had a wife in Russia."

"You think."

"Bet this is her stuff." Heather reached deeper into the trunk; as she pulled items out to view, she paused. "The side is loose."

Roman looked. "It's not loose. It's a compartment."

"No way," Heather said with excitement. "A secret compartment?"

Roman nodded.

"He's got something in here. Maybe my mom is right."

Roman paused. "Stop. She is not. It's just …" The side flap folded over as if it were supposed to. Silver cases were revealed, no bigger than four inches. They lined against the case.

"Drugs?" Heather asked.

"No way."

"Should we open one?"

Roman hesitated. "Bet it's money or gold."

"Oh, he's probably worth a fortune. And you just aren't supposed to know. Go on."

Roman pulled out one of the cases. He opened it, and inside were six silver tubes that looked exactly like cigarettes. Same size, shape, in fact, they were made that way, down to the part that resembled a filter.

"What are they? Just metal cigarettes. Oh my God, Roman, your dad invented the first E cigarette."

"Weird." Roman lifted one. He touched the mimicked filter end and it turned. "Oh wow."

"Drugs." Heather nodded. "Or secret scrolls."

Roman took off the filter and taped it on his hand. "Nothing. Just this." He pulled out a wire. The size of a Q-tip. Straight on one end, the other was a small glass coil. "Son of a bitch, you're right. He invented the first electronic cigarette. Wow."

"Kind of a letdown." Heather said.

"Yeah, but …" Roman stopped when he heard the footsteps above them.

"Roman?" The woman's voice called out. "Are you here?"

Roman cleared his throat. "Be right up."

"Shit. Vivian." Heather cringed. "You think she'll tell your dad?"

"No, but let's get back up there."

Hurriedly, as a team, they returned things to the way they were, or so they thought. In their haste, they neglected to notice two things.

One, Roman never replaced the key.

The other … when he hurriedly replaced the coil back into the metal tube, he never noticed that he broke the tip of the glass spiral.

FLASH FORWARD

Ground Zero – 4

December 23rd

Hartworth, Montana

For the first time in his career, Edward had to pause to throw up, and then he downed a drink. His examination of Vivian Morris went about as far as it could go before he got sick. It wasn't just the sight and smell of her, it was the thought of what had occurred.

"I need an investigative team," Edward told Dr. Lange, head of the Centers for Disease Control in his first telephone conversation to headquarters. "Body removal and another team of virologists. We have to trace this thing. We need to find out exactly what it is."

"You've only been there three hours, Ed. What in the hell …"

"Over eight hundred bodies. One just thawed enough for me to examine … my God, Bill." Edward grabbed his flask. "This woman … these people … this … thing. I'm scared to death."

At first, his soft laugh carried over the line, then Dr. Bill Lange breathed outward. "You're very serious."

"Yes. Yes, I am. Bill." Edward paused to take a sip. "I don't even know if *I'll* end up with it, for as much precaution as I've taken. This thing is like nothing I have ever seen. Nothing. And it's fast, my God, is it fast. Last phone call out of this town was placed a few days ago; that's when I guess the town died."

"When did it hit there? Any guesses?"

"No more than a week."

"Jesus."

"Tell me about it," Edward said. "I just did my first examination, and I got sick. Sick, Bill. Underneath what was left of her skin … and I say what was left because the victim either scratched her skin away or it tore from within. And what was beneath it … it was like tar, looked like tar and smelled like bile. Everything inside was destroyed. Internal organs barely recognizable. They were mush. If there was any blood left in the victim's body, it was too thick to run through the veins and just seeped through any bodily orifice it could find."

"Where … where did it start?" Dr. Lange asked. "Any idea?"

"I'd be guessing," Edward replied. "But I'd say it was inhaled. Maybe it started as a respiratory ailment, who knows, but it hit the digestive system and ate through it like acid."

"Septicemia?"

Edward laughed. "We need a new word for it. Trust me. Septicemia is a walk in a park compared to this. And you know what the worst part is?"

"There's worse?" Dr. Lange asked.

"Oh, yeah. The brain. Barely touched. That tells me the victim knew every single thing that was happening to them. This woman felt every single ounce of pain and sickness, and my guess is she went through an agony that was inhumane."

"I'm disbursing as many units as I can to you. They'll be there by the end of the day," Dr. Lange said. "Have you tried the neighboring communities?"

"I am keeping the State Police at bay and out of those towns just in case. I'm scared. There's a town thirty miles north of here, one forty miles east. The last phone call went to Lincoln. Those are small towns. But Billings … it's only ninety miles away."

"This hit fast; do you think it broke boundaries?" Dr. Lange asked.

"It should have under normal circumstances," Edward said. "But these aren't normal. You have everyday folks, dead cowboys in pickup trucks with shotguns on every single road leading in and out of town. This makes me wonder if there is a BSL-4 lab around here. Maybe a resident here brought in the germ, knew it was released, and they shut down and sealed in the town. Set up an aid station, prepared for it. Kept it down until everyone died."

"Someone knew it was this bad?"

"Without a doubt. My only hope is they shut down this town fast enough." At that instant, Edward's eye lifted to the opening of the lab door. "My team just returned. Let me call you back."

Dr. Lange told him he was assembling more teams, and the conversation ended.

Using the intercom, Edward told Harold to double disinfect, then waited for him to walk into the office portion.

He knew by the look on Harold's face that he had more information.

"We found a whole bunch of bodies," Harold said. "Maybe a eighty or more."

"There's eight hundred plus people in this town, of …"

"No." Harold stopped him. "Let me finish. We found a bunch of bodies. Apparently infected … but they didn't die of our sickness. They were shot."

Edward was barreled over by the news. "It can't be."

"Single shot to the head. Men, women, children."

"Someone finished off the town."

Harold shook his head. "Nope. Someone killed the people who weren't going to die from the illness."

Edward ran his hand down his face with a hard sigh. "What the hell? Why?"

With his question came a thump on his desk. Harold tossed a sealed bag; in it was what looked like a journal."

"What is it?" Edward asked.

"Your answers," Harold replied. "Someone documented everything. I only skimmed through, but I'm pretty certain," he pointed to the journal, "that right there solves the mystery of what happened to this town."

Chapter Six

Hartworth, Montana

December 16th

Vivian Morris was done for the day. She thanked Bonnie for the pie she brought with her at her appointment and apologized for the wait. But Bonnie was the last patient of the day. Vivian cleaned up the waiting area, pulled the charts for the next day, and powered down the computer.

As she did a sneeze reverberated through her entire body. “Oh man,” she said out loud. “I hope I didn’t catch what Mr. Stevens had. Jeez.” After rubbing a tissue under her nose, she told herself it was just some dust, and grabbed her coat.

“Dr. Paltrov,” she called out. “Dr. Paltrov.”

“In my office,” he replied.

Vivian stepped to his office door. “I’m leaving. I’ll see you in the morning. Everything is shut down.”

“Thank you.” He nodded as he sat behind his desk. He looked tired and worn; then again, he was pushing seventy and put in long hours. “Vivian, did my son call while I was with patients?”

"No, he didn't." she replied. "They probably, got there, checked in, then headed to the concert."

"More than likely. Thank you."

"Goodnight." She started to leave and paused when she felt a draft come from the other hall. She peered down, saw the culprit then popped her head back into the doctor's office. "The basement door is opened, it's bringing a draft. Want me to close it?"

"The basement door is … is open?" He questioned.

Vivian nodded.

"No, I will get it. Thank you."

"No problem, good night," she said again, pulled the door closed, and walked out.

Val listened to the sounds of her leaving and stood up immediately. He didn't recall leaving the basement open when he left for his rounds a few hours earlier. He was so busy when he returned he never thought about it, but Val had to check it out.

The light was off, but the door indeed was ajar.

Val began to close it and paused. He decided to go to the basement and check on things. He knew the second he reached the bottom of the staircase that his things had been touched.

The largest of the trunks had been moved and with a groan and a chest full of worry, Val raced to the trunk and opened it. He begged in his mind that everything was fine. But it wasn't. It was apparent the side compartment, covered by the lining, had been opened.

One by one he took out the silver cases. One by one he opened them, pulled out each tube within and carefully examined each one. On the sixth case, second tube, he knew.

He just knew.

He uncapped it and pulled out the small wire.

The instant he saw it, his stomach dropped and every ounce of his being froze. Val dropped further to the floor and wept out a single heart aching sob of defeat as he stared at the broken glass spiral.

There was only one person who could have been down there touching the trunk.

One person with enough curiosity.

That person was his son, Roman. His only child, the only family member he had since his wife died.

God help him, Val thought, if it was Roman.

No. He closed his eyes tighter. God help everyone.

◇◇◇◇

Billings, Montana

Heather wished she could rip her nose from her face and breathe a little easier. She couldn't believe how fast her nose clogged. It wasn't running, it was just stuffed.

She started getting a tickle in her throat right after they stopped for fast food, then her stomach knotted.

It was turning into the worst cold she'd ever had.

She felt horrible.

By the time she got to the hotel, she'd caught a chill she couldn't shake. Roman was already complaining he was getting a cold, too.

"Swell," she said to him. "Just swell. The first time we get away and we're both sick."

"But we aren't missing the concert," he told her. "Not this one."

They both showered. Heather lay on the bed and rested while Roman cleaned up. The shower helped a little, but not as much as the bourbon they packed.

The both did a double shot before heading to the concert hall.

The venue was so packed they had to park three blocks away. It was cold, and Heather could barely walk by the time they made it to the venue property.

Things were worse there. So many people headed toward the doors that they were packed in like sardines. Pushed and shoved, pushed and shoved. Heather tried to tell Roman she was getting worse, but he looked as if he were in a fog as well.

Finally, after her head spun, a wave of nausea hit Heather, and she broke free of the pack of people, just far enough away to vomit.

Her body shook and heaved, and people groaned out, shouted, and laughed.

Knees buckling, Heather dropped to the sidewalk. Roman hurried to her.

She looked up to him. "I think I have food poisoning."

"Me, too, I'm really sick," he said. "I think we should go back to the hotel."

Heather nodded, tried to stand, and fell back down.

"Hey!" a man yelled. "Get your drunk ass girlfriend out of here!"

"She's not drunk, she's sick." Roman grabbed hold of her arm. "She's sick."

Heather knew the walk to the truck would seem enormous. But she knew once she got there, it wouldn't be long before she got to the hotel and went straight to bed.

That was all Heather could think about.

Sleep.

◇◇◇◇

Val called Roman nine times. Not once did he answer.

He hadn't left his office since he discovered the trunk had been opened. He physically was sweating it out, praying with everything he had that Roman was spared.

He knew what was released.

He even called Vivian.

"Do you remember, Vivian, if Roman was in the basement?"

"Is everything okay?" she asked.

"Yes, yes, I just want to make sure it was Roman and not someone else."

"I promised him I wouldn't tell you, but yeah, they were. They …" she paused to sneeze.

The sound of her sneeze went through Val like a bullet. "Are you okay?"

"I'm fine, just coming down with a cold."

After hesitation, he told her to take care and again he thanked her. No sooner did Val hang up, he sunk his face into his hands. Vivian was at the office all day, the basement door open, the draft blowing from below. Not just Vivian but all the patients who came into the office after three. The waiting room was packed.

"Oh God." Val closed his eyes. He tried Roman once more. No answer. Then Val knew what he had to do.

◇◇◇◇

While it wasn't even nine PM, Sheriff Lawrence Meadows was getting ready for bed. After all, he had to be at work at five AM. He had a night cap, packed his lunch for the next day, and was in the middle of turning off the lights when the steady knocking started at his door.

His immediate thought was that there was an emergency at the station, but if there was, surely someone would have called.

His Ty-Bow flannel was open around his tee shirt, and the man of fifty, in decent shape, walked to the door. "Doc."

Val took off his hat, and hurriedly stepped inside. "We have a problem, Larry."

His insides shook. Without knowing specifics, without hearing what the problem was, the sheriff was pretty certain he knew what the doctor referred to. Almost as if he waited thirty-five years for the knock at the door.

He knew the day was coming, he just hoped it wasn't in his lifetime.

Larry shut the door. "What … what is the problem?"

Val only turned and faced him. His expression said it all.

"Jesus," Larry gasped out. "When?"

"It had to be while I was making rounds. Between one and three this afternoon."

"Oh my God." Larry swiped his hand down his face, walked to the fireplace mantel, and grabbed his bottle. He poured a drink.

"This day … we hoped would never come."

"We knew it would." Larry downed his drink and poured another. "Who?"

"Roman."

Larry closed his eyes. "Maybe he won't get sick. You said, I remember years ago, that in a few decades it would lose potency and be nothing and then we could get rid of it."

"Enough time has not passed."

"Did you inoculate him?" Larry asked.

Val shook his head. "I only had four doses. I gave my wife the last one. And the three other people ...Your father, you and your nephew."

A lump formed in Larry's throat. He remembered that day, getting the shot. He was told it was a shot like tetanus. That was the day the trunks were moved into the storage compartment of his father's barn, the only heated barn in the county. Val was younger then, new to America, and gave his father fifty thousand dollars to store the case. His father was a farmer but wasn't stupid. He knew something wasn't right about the cases. But the money saved the farm, and his father never said a word. Larry later learned that out of gratefulness, Val gave the father and Larry the inoculation. He also inoculated Larry's nephew, his sister's little boy, because he knew how much Larry's father idolized and lived for the child. Just on the outside chance that anything happened with the case, Val wanted to be certain the family survived. At least some of them.

That was thirty-five years earlier. Since then, his father had passed, the nephew moved away, and the farm since sold.

When did Larry learn the contents of the trunk?

He was in his twenties, just started working for the State Police, and, while visiting his father's farm, his curiosity, like Roman's got the best of him.

He never really knew what was in the trunk. He bluffed Val. Bluffed and blackmailed him. By doing so, Val told him the contents. Larry, by knowing the contents, was just as guilty as Val.

Over the years a friendship formed, a bond by a secret they both vowed to protect.

Val had smuggled the germ when he worked as a scientist. He didn't smuggle it for bad reasons, but to keep it out of bad hands. Val always told Larry, if they knew where it was, no one could misuse it. The world was safe as long as they protected it.

They never wanted to bury it, because they feared someone would find it.

It was a heat resistant virus; burning the liquid virus would only multiply the germ and send it into the air, making it even more of a weapon than it already was.

Instead, they watched the cases constantly. Had perfect storage for them. No extreme variations of temperatures that could cause the fragile glass that contained the virus to break.

The plan was simple; since they were both immune by the inoculation, they would protect the case. After Val's death, Larry would hold responsibility.

Eventually the virus would die.

But Larry knew and never worried about the case or something happening to them before the germ died. A part of him always feared the accidental release.

And it happened.

"How is Roman now?" Larry asked.

Val shook his head. "I don't know. I haven't heard from him. He and Heather went to Billings for a concert."

"A concert?" Larry shrieked. "Oh my God."

Val held up his hand. “They are immediate ground zero. More than likely they were feeling it by the time they left. They were to check in the hotel. My guess, they never left the room.”

“The check in clerk …”

“He is still on duty there. I called to see if they checked in and he had said that he personally checked them and they were the last ones to check in.”

“Still, it’s a hotel.”

“Actually a motel. Not a big one nor busy, but that is not my concern. That can be handled.” Val said. “This town is my concern now. Roman and Heather are immediate ground zero, but there are other ground zero patients. Anyone who came into the clinic, wave one. Any building within a one mile radius of my clinic. This thing is fast, Larry. Initial exposed will feel flu-like symptoms tomorrow. Contact victims the next day. It’s Monday. By Wednesday not a person in this town will be well enough to walk down the street. Friday they’ll start dying if they’re not already dead.”

“Jesus Christ, we have to call the authorities. Call the health department, CDC, whatever …”

“No. We can’t do that and you know it.”

“What?” Larry laughed in ridicule. “Why the hell not?”

“The people in this town may not know it, but they’re already dead. Every man, woman and child. You and I will be the only ones standing. Then we’ll stand trial. We will be the men that go down in history as the ones who released the world's deadliest biological weapon. Accident or not."

Larry poured another drink, downed it, and brought his hands to his head. "My God, this isn't happening. If we don't call them, we can't help the people."

"We can't help them anyhow."

"What do we do?"

"The only thing we can. This town is far enough removed. Very few outsiders come in. This thing is only going to take a few days. We do the only thing we can. Sit down right now, devise a story, and devise a plan. We have a chance at stopping this thing here and now. Stopping it from spreading. But we have to act fast," Val said. "We have no choice. We have to shut down. We have to seal the town."

Chapter Seven

Lincoln, Montana

December 16th

Andy wasn't gone all that long from Emma's, maybe a half an hour, but it was long enough for Del to get to the house after he saw Andy in town.

His car was parked in the driveway, angled as always to stop a car from pulling in next to him. Where did he think he was, at a mall?

Since Del was on his extended visit, he was always at the house. Andy didn't let it bother him too much, he just hung around Emma who avoided Del. Del was there for Richie or Heather. Seldom Cody. It was as if he refused to recognize Cody as a grandchild.

After parking his truck, Andy walked around to the back and lifted the bushel basket from the rear. He carried it with him up the driveway to the house and stepped inside.

Andy could have predicted what he'd see.

Del and Richie in the living room, the standard pizza box, empty soda cans tossed about as they played video games. They used a white board to communicate.

After three weeks, Andy thought for sure Del would have learned to sign some.

He tapped Richie on the head to let him know he was there. "I'm back; I'll be in the kitchen." Andy signed. "Hand me a slice?"

"Sure thing," Richie replied and grabbed a piece of pizza for Andy.

Del paused in playing. "Hey, nice basket of tomatoes."

Richie signed, "I thought you were dropping them off at Bonnie's diner."

"I was," Andy signed. "But she was gone early tonight. They must not have been busy. You having fun?"

"Yeah, actually, I kinda like him more now."

Andy laughed.

"Ok, enough," Del said. "I know you guys are talking about me."

"N … not every … every th… thing is about you-you."

"Re….re…really."

Andy sighed and walked out.

From the kitchen Emma yelled, "I heard that, Andy. You have my permission to deck him. It is my house."

Andy ignored her typical statement and looked at Del. "We .. we were t … talking about you." Andy stumbled over the 'R', then skipped it and said, "He … he … likes being with … with you."

Del smiled, grabbed a pen and wrote down what Andy said. He showed it to Richie.

Richie nodded.

"Cool." Del grinned. "Let's hang out more. You can go continue to be an errand boy for Emma, Andy, she's in the kitchen."

Thinking 'he's such an asshole' but not saying it, Andy went into the kitchen. He set the bushel on the floor. "B … B … closed."

"Really?" Emma asked. "That's odd. She must have been dead in the diner tonight." After a shrug, she thanked Andy and kissed him. "I appreciate you going down there. We'll just take it tomorrow. Right now, prepping these tomatoes for canning is a bitch."

"I … t … told you. N-not to start tonight."

"I know. But now I won't be happy until we finish." She peered over Cody's shoulder. "Oh, honey, good job."

Cody held a plastic knife, pretending to peel the tomato, but she smashed it more than anything.

Andy grabbed a paper towel. As he wiped the child's hands, the back door opened.

Stew walked in.

"Dad?" Emma said surprised. "What the heck are you doing here at this hour?"

"I just finished my poker game and I remembered what I had to tell you this morning."

"Really?" Emma asked. "What's that?"

"The other …" Stew paused. "Why does the baby have a knife?"

"It's plastic and play. She's fine. We're canning."

"At nine thirty at night?" Stew asked.

"I started and can't stop until I get a good grip on things. What do you have to tell me?"

"I was saying …" Stew paused. "Holy shit." He walked to the bushel of tomatoes. "Where in the hell did all this come from? They're ripe." He grabbed one and sniffed. "Perfect. Where are you getting homegrown tomatoes in December?"

"Um ... the hole." Emma said.

Andy explained further. "She … g … g … grew them."

"Hydroponics," Emma boasted. "And you said I wasted my education."

"I still think that," Stew said. "But good job on the tomatoes."

"Yeah, well, we have a ton. I over-planted." Emma shrugged then changed the tone of her voice to a higher pitch as she focused her words to Cody. "So we're canning. We'll be eating tons of tomatoes in the apocalypse." She cleared her throat. "My estimate. I can eat a jar a day for over a year."

"Swell," Stew said. "I'm sure the tomatoes in the apocalypse will come in handy. You still have this bushel to do?"

Emma shook her head. "Nah. I'm giving that to Bonnie. Andy took it down, but she was closed."

"Closed?" Stew asked. "That's a surprise. The diner must have been dead."

Andy nodded.

"Dad? What did you wanna tell me?"

Stew opened his mouth and paused. “Goddamn it. I forgot.”

“Must have not been important,” Emma said.

“It was important.” Stew winced. “I think.”

“Maybe it was a lie.”

Stew huffed. “Now why the hell would I come down to your house to tell you a lie?”

“You’re old. You have nothing better to do than to bother your grown daughter.”

Andy reached over and gave a playful nudge to Emma. “Be … b … be nice.”

Emma giggled.

“I come here to make sure my grown daughter isn’t corrupting my great-granddaughter.”

“Too late.” Emma smiled. “Did you wanna stay?”

“Nah, I’m gonna go. Asshole’s here and I’d rather not see him.” Stew looked at Andy. “Did you deck him yet?”

Emma answered, “Unfortunately, not yet. He will.”

“I doubt it. Andy’s too nice.” Stew grabbed the bushel. “And so am I. I’ll take this for you in the morning when I go to Bonnie’s for breakfast.”

“Thanks,” Emma told him.

“You .. you .. you sure?” Andy asked.

“Absolutely.” Stew kissed Cody, then Emma, and walked to the door. “Oh. Hey. Have you heard from Heather?”

“Is that what you wanted to tell me or ask?”

Stew shook his head. "No. I'll remember eventually. But I was curious about Heather. I haven't heard from her since I got a text when she arrived."

"That's when I heard from her. She's probably at the concert having a great time. No worries," Emma said. "Everything is fine."

◇◇◇◇

Billings, Montana

The wrenching, twisting, and burning pain in her stomach caused Heather to jolt awake. She wanted to jump from the bed but couldn't move, so she leaned over the side of the bed and vomited into the awaiting garbage can.

"Roman," she weakly called out. The vomit tasted different. It smelled different. It had an iron flavor to it as she wiped her mouth with the back of her hand. "Roman," she called again then reached up for the light. When she did, the light brightened the room and also the smear of blood on her hand. "Oh God," she panicked.

Roman sat up on the other bed. Every cover wrapped around him and his body visually shivered. "Heather, I'm so sick."

"Me, too. Something is wrong. My skin is burning. It feels like it's on fire, and it itches."

Roman removed his arm from the cover and extended it to Heather. "I was scratching in my sleep."

Heather looked at the purple splotches on his arm. It was swollen, and scratches covered every inch of his forearm. "Call your dad. We need help."

◇◇◇◇

Val grew tired of waiting and was already on his way to Billings when he received the phone call from Roman.

They were sick, so sick they wanted to go to the hospital. Val told them to hang tight, he was on the way. He explained on the phone that someone from another town brought in a very bad case of a stomach flu, but all would be fine. He was certain that Roman understood.

He made it to the hotel within a half hour of the call. It was a single story, truck stop motel just off the freeway.

Three of the rooms were lit, and there were only a couple of cars in the lot. That was a good sign.

Val was ready; he arrived prepared and knew what he had to do. He parked next to Roman's car. Before he went to their room, he walked into the motel office.

No one was there. He hit the bell, waited, and then a younger man came from the back room. He looked Middle Eastern and smiled at Val. "You need a room."

"I'm looking for my son. I spoke to a man earlier who said he arrived here safely. My son's name is Roman Paltrov."

"Oh, yes. That was me. You spoke to me," the man said then stopped to sneeze.

"Bless you."

"Thank you."

"And you have been here all day since they checked in?"

"Yeah. Listen, Mister, policy won't let me tell you the room number. I can call for you, though. Ring him." He asked.

"That won't be necessary. You've been very helpful."

"Anything else I can do for you?"

"No, you've told me all I need to know." Cold, without thought, without emotion, Val reached into his coat. He pulled out a revolver with a silencer already attached, aimed the weapon, and before the motel man could react, Val fired.

A single shot to the man's head.

Quickly, Val left the office, walked down eight doors to Roman's room and knocked. There wasn't an answer and the door was unlocked.

The stench was ungodly when Val walked in and he huffed an exhalation from his nostrils. Roman reached out his hand to Val, and Heather lay on her side. She struggled to lift her head.

He said nothing. Approaching Heather first, he wrapped her in the bed's blanket and lifted her into his arms.

"My mom. I want my mom."

"Let's get you out of here first," Val said.

Heather's head fell to his chest. "I'm so sick."

"I know."

He carried her out and placed her in the back of his car, then returned for Roman. He was too heavy to carry, so he had to help his son out.

It broke Val's heart to see his son so sick and nothing that he could do for him. As he placed him in the back next to Heather, Val leaned close to his only child. "I am very sorry. I am so sorry." He kissed his son on the forehead. The heat of Roman's skin stung his lips.

He closed the door, walked around to the back of the car and opened the trunk. From it he pulled two small gas cans and walked back to the room. He visually scanned it, grabbed Roman's wallet from the table and Heather's purse. He then took the first gas can and doused the entire contents about the room.

The second gas can was reserved for Roman's car.

After he emptied, connecting a trail of gas into a puddle just outside the room, he placed the containers, Heather's purse, and the wallet in the trunk, got in the car and pulled twenty feet from the spot.

Leaving it running, he placed it in park, lit a cigarette, stepped out of the car, walked closer to the motel, and hit the smoke once.

He watched the red ambers ignite, and then he tossed it. As soon as he saw it started a flame, Val hurriedly returned to the car, shut the door, and drove off.

"It will be alright," Val told them. "I promise. A couple days it will be over. It's just a bad bug." He peeked in the rear view mirror to make sure his attempts at destruction were successful.

They were.

Burning the liquid host virus would be detrimental, but Val was positive burning the germ from the infected would destroy it and that's what he did.

Destroyed the germs they left behind.

Driving off, the 'boom' of an explosion rang out, and Val kept driving without incident. Heather and Roman were far too ill to notice that the motel they had just left was completely engulfed in flames.

FLASH FORWARD

Ground Zero – 5

December 23rd

Hartworth, Montana

'In my own mind, in my own way, I believed I was saving the world. If I watched it, I protected it, then no one could get it and all would be safe. I suppose it was an accident waiting to happen. Like a loose piece of carpet on the stairs that never gets fixed, eventually it trips you. But now, I make one more valiant effort.'

"Christ," Edward muttered after reading the first words in the makeshift journal, a paragraph scribbled on the first page of the book. Inside were pages of documentations, notes of what was done, what happened. Had it not included the eerie first paragraph then Edward would have believed a caretaker took the notes.

That epitaph to the journal of the dead told Edward the responsible party wrote it.

However, the responsible party conveniently left out his or her name and, from a quick skim, nothing to indicate what it was. Only a number was given, and that told Edward very little.

The journal started … *'December 17th, Midnight. There are two patient zeros, both present at the time of release. Nine hours post exposure. Steady fever of 103. Vomiting has lessened, but now consists of bile laced with blood. Patients complain of severe skin discomfort. No visual lesions other than self inflicted. Both patient one and two are alert and conscious of what is occurring. I am positive there are no contact victims connected to these two patients. However, I have accounted for twelve individuals who were in the vicinity in the post release of EPV-571. I am confident that patient three, Vivian, will experience the same within twelve hours. I will visit her in a few to check.'*

Edward wanted to highlight a few items, but the notebook was sealed and he'd have to take it into the lab to do so, so he jotted down his thoughts and dropped his pencil.

"Anything?" Harold asked when he walked in.

"Other than this goes to prove you never know who your neighbors are?" Edward replied. "We have a title on the germ. EPV-571. We'll start there. Have CDC and WHO run it. If it's in the database, then it may have a cure or antidote. Obviously, this is an experimental germ that someone in this town was working on or had in their possession."

"Who the hell would do that?" Harold asked.

"Scientist. Doctor. Lab worker. Stole it. Hid it here. This is cowboy land. They could have put on their best hat and pretended, for all we know. But Vivian's name is mentioned. She was at ground zero after the release."

"That's something to go by." Harold pulled up a chair. "Check this out. Martha and I were hitting up the social media sites."

"And?"

"Apparently this wasn't all that hush-hush. We did a public post search, hashtags, were able to find about a dozen posts about the quarantine. Sent the links to headquarters for them to dig deeper; we can only see so much because we don't have a 'friend' connection." He pushed papers forward. "I printed them up."

Edward read a few of them.

'Sealed in Hartworth. Scary shit. I'm not coming out.'

The other posts he read reiterated that sentiment.

Harold said, "Martha right now is working with the basic white pages to get an address on some of these names. Maybe we can check the houses."

"Good call. How the hell do people post on social media and this thing not get out?"

Harold shrugged. "My best guess would be that the people in the three towns that posted were just a handful of people. They were probably told to keep quiet. But they posted anyhow, and you're talking a combined population of less than three thousand people. A dozen or so important posts buried beneath and lost under stupid cartoons and everyday garbage. These people cried out. No one heard them. When they did … it was already too late. Last posts by these people were days ago."

Edward looked down to his watch. "Okay, we have about four more hours until this whole area is overrun with CDC, WHO, military, you name it. Then after that, maybe another two hours before this thing goes public, no matter how hard we try to keep a lid on it. Hopefully, headquarters will nail what it is by the slides I sent and this code … EPV-571. Until then, we need to come up with viable answers as to what happened here. Those answers all start here." He pulled forth the notebook.

Chapter Seven

Hartworth, Montana

December 17th

Val barely slept, but he supposed that was nothing compared to what Roman and Heather were experiencing. Around three in the morning he delivered a strong sedative to both of them. He stashed away what he had at the clinic. He'd save it for them so they could sleep through most of what they endured.

He prayed. Val hadn't done that since his wife passed away, yet he pulled out his rosary beads and prayed for them. He knew there was no saving the young people, he knew he was going to lose his son, but he prayed for a quick end and for minimum agony.

It was just about time to begin. He heard Larry outside earlier, preparing the streets. Val recorded a new voicemail, because if all went the way he envisioned, he'd have a clinic full by late in the day.

The flier would be passed out to every single home. They were already posted on the telephone poles.

They were playing the role of reverse psychology on people, telling them through the flier that there had been unconfirmed rumors of a horrible outbreak outside of Hartworth, and to keep everyone safe from infection, they were shutting down the town for three days. Asking everyone for their cooperation.

Of course, they would tell the ill a completely different story. Val knew the ill wouldn't be able to do much after a day. Also, Val and Larry figured, by the time everyone started to get sick, they'd be far too sick to leave or even worry about it.

Scare them into staying put, not wanting to leave, and keeping people out.

Val imagined several of the town's men hooting out an excited, 'Hell yeah, we'll take post and guard our town,' unaware of the truth.

Would it work?

It only remained to be seen.

Just before five, the designated kickoff time, Val checked on Roman and Heather once more. He grabbed a clipboard and left.

He and Larry were starting the daunting task of going door to door.

◇◇◇◇

There were pretty much only two ways into Hartworth. Every other road, including the dirt roads from the ranches and the highway exits, emptied on to that four-lane, state-maintained road that went straight through town..

Larry had doubled up on things. He placed two roadblocks a half mile outside of Hartworth on the east and west side, then a second truck only fifty feet inside the city limits.

Shutting down Hartworth was easy. Keeping people calm wouldn't be a problem, as long as they were scared and followed the rules.

Hartworth residents were isolated as it was.

The problem was with the ranchers. Larry paid a visit to those six homes before he started the roadblocks. He informed them to stay put, not let anyone on their property, and if they could, just avoid town for a few days.

They seemed, to him, to be more than willing to listen. Not much interested in the internet, they took his word of the brain virus as gospel.

After informing his men on post on what to do, Larry resumed his door to door task.

He didn't expect much traffic coming into town, but the most would come from the east, and Larry himself would take that post once he was finished with the houses. He'd take the busy time, as he called it, when traders came though along with deliveries.

Larry would divert them and hopefully do so without word spreading.

◇◇◇◇

Vivian couldn't breathe though her nose. It was the worst cold she ever recalled having. It wasn't even slurpy sluggish when she breathed, it was hitting a brick mucus wall.

Nothing.

She ached, and she knew she had a fever. She hated the fact that she promised Roman she'd fill in for him and now she was going to have to call in sick.

Vivian probably would have stayed in bed had it not been for that knot in her stomach.

She tried to vomit, but it was futile; she only gagged. The skin on her right hand was burning as if it were in the beginning stages of a rash.

She hated to do it, but she had to call off of work. She could barely make it to the stairs, let alone the office. She paused by the door of each of her children's rooms. Her daughter slept soundly, but her son was restless, tossing and coughing.

Poor thing, she thought, they must have both caught it from the same source.

As she headed to the stairs to retrieve her phone on the first floor, her husband Darrell called to her.

"Viv? You okay?"

"Yeah," she coughed. "Really sick. Go back to sleep. I'm gonna lay on the couch."

"You need anything?"

"No. Just sleep. Thanks." She walked slowly down the stairs. Her plan was to get a drink and call the doc, but she only made it to the bottom of the stairs when she heard a knock on the door.

It wasn't even six in the morning; who would be knocking, she thought.

She peeked through the drape.

Doc?

Vivian opened the door. "Doc?"

His eyes cased her up and down. "Oh, Vivian. Are you ill?"

"Yes, I was just getting ready to call you. What's going on?"

"Vivian, the town is under quarantine," Val spoke softly. "We believe a man from Omaha brought something into the town, so we are taking precautions."

Vivian's hand shot to her mouth. "Do I have it?"

"You may. I'll need to examine you," Val said. "We are asking all those who may be infected to come to the fire hall and stay clear of those who are not ill. Can you do that?"

Vivian nodded. "I'll get my things and be right there. Should I be worried?"

"No. No, not at all." Val waved out his hand. "It'll be over in a few days."

Vivian thanked Val. He turned and left and she closed the door. She felt horrible, and a quarantine in town was frightening. But Vivian felt better knowing she only had to suffer just a couple days.

<><><><>

Heather had never been so sick in all of her life.

She vomited the last bit that was left in her stomach, and it felt as if there were a hole in her abdomen, a vague nothingness that knotted and pulled.

Her skin hurt, worse than any sunburn she ever had in her life.

Choking on something, Heather woke from a sound sleep. She didn't know what it was that choked her, but it was gone. She was groggy but managed to roll out of bed. Standing was a chore. She had to hold on to everything to stand and balance. Roman was still sleeping in the single bed next to her.

Heather wasn't a doctor, but she was smart enough to know something was wrong. Dreadfully wrong.

Why did Val not take them to a hospital? She looked down at her forearms. They were black. Not purple or splotched, black as if they were rotting. Roman was worse. His face was black, his neck swollen.

She was certain, without a doubt, that she'd vomited blood, but it was dark. Surely, Val had to see the severity in that.

About four steps from the bed, Heather started to cry. She could barely walk. Her thoughts were on her daughter. Her baby girl. How she wanted to see her and hold her again. And Heather thought of her mother. Even though she was a woman, she felt like a little girl, so desperately needing to hear her mother's voice, to feel her mother's arms.

Where was she? Did she not know she was ill?

Maybe not.

Maybe Val never told her mom.

A noise outside caught Heather's attention, and she weakly made her way to the window. She parted the drapes to peek out. It was barely light out yet the street was busy.

The second story window allotted her the vantage point of seeing the fire hall two streets over. People walked slowly in there. A fire truck flashed its light as if it was a beacon.

Heather didn't have much energy left in her. What she did have she was going to use to the fullest extent.

She had to find the phone and call her mother.

FLASH FORWARD

Ground Zero – 6

December 23rd

Hartworth, Montana

“How in the world does a town just shut down?” Edward questioned as he sat with Harold, going through the journal.

“This is something we can’t put together before everyone arrives, you know that,” Harold said. “We can try. But it’s a lot.”

Edward shook his head. “They lied to the people of this town. Half the people thought some brain virus making everyone crazy was infecting the world, and the other half knew there was an illness in Hartworth. How did they pull it off?”

“The ill were too sick to care, and the ones hiding didn’t believe anyone,” Harold guessed. “Martha finished the fire hall body count.”

“And?”

“Two hundred and twenty.”

Edward rubbed his eyes. “Which means that people are in their homes.”

"There are a lot of gunshot victims, self-inflicted as well."

"This man … or woman," Edward pointed to the journal, "is the one we need to find. Who wrote this?"

"He's more than likely dead."

"I know. Any word from Martha on the last phone call? It was placed on the 20th."

"She's looking for him now. We don't know this town. She and Dickson should have some answers soon," Harold said.

"Maybe our caller was the journal keeper," Edward guessed. "He or she thought they were saving the world. They believed the quarantine would work. Listen to this …" Edward read. "*December 17th, four PM. We have secured perimeters. No one has entered or left town. I believe this is contained. At this point we have checked in over one hundred people at the fire hall. I believe these are initial ground zero release victims. As long as no one at ground zero left town we are good. Like the measles or conjunctivitis, EPV-571 is not contagious until the onset of symptoms. Problem is, when do the symptoms actually start? What is the initial symptom? It could be a sneeze, a cough, or a chill. That is the scary part.*' Edward stopped reading.

"Whoever wrote the journal has full knowledge of the bug and had it before the release."

"Agreed," Edward said.

"So why did they write the journal?"

"That's the easiest question to answer," Edward replied. "For us. For those who found the town. To know what happened. To let us know what it was and what it does. To know this virus. I think they did it just in case it broke the barriers."

Harold pointed to the notebook. "They knew the bug well. I think we're good. Small town. Isolated. The germ moves so fast it kills its host before the host can infect anyone. In hindsight, one day was all the town needed to be shut down; after that, keeping the people in here was effortless because all were infected. I'm optimistic, Edward, that it didn't leave this town."

"I hope you're right," Edward said, glancing to Harold. "Because God help us if it did."

Chapter Eight

Lincoln, Montana

December 17th

Not that Stew minded bringing that bushel of tomatoes into Bonnie's Diner, he wouldn't have offered if he did, but he did mind the fact that the door was open and not a soul was in there. Coffee was made, pastries were out, but there wasn't a waitress or Bonnie around.

He put the bushel in the back, calling out as he did.

No answer.

He stepped behind the counter. The grills were warm, the coffee smelled fresh, but no one was around to cook or take orders.

The bell above the door caught his attention.

"You cooking today?" asked the male patron in a joking manner.

"No, I'm a little curious where everyone is. The diner is open and Bonnie isn't here."

"Maybe she ran home."

"Maybe." Stew poured a cup of coffee for himself and one for the man who sat at the counter. "It's still early." Holding his coffee, he pulled his phone from his pocket. Still no word from Heather. He was starting to worry.

"Can you put the television on?" the man asked. "Remote's near the toaster."

"Sure thing." Stew grabbed the remote, clicked on the set, put the remote before the man, and walked around to the patron side of the diner and slid onto a stool. The moment he did, the news caught his attention. A blazing fire, but Stew couldn't make out what they were saying.

"Damn shame," the man said. "Hear it's arson. Entire motel in Billings went up. No one lived."

Stew's eyes widened. "That's in Billings."

"Little trucker style motel."

Stew wasn't certain what motel or hotel Heather stayed at, but immediately he jumped from his seat, tossed money on the counter, and flew out the door.

He hoped and prayed the entire way to Emma's that the fire wasn't the reason he hadn't heard from Heather. He didn't know what he would do if that were the case.

◇◇◇◇

Del's hand tapped on the steering wheel to the beat of the song. It was a catchy tune, a rough draft, a demo submitted by the songwriters. Del loved it.

He turned down the volume and lifted his phone. He hit re-dial on the last call he placed. Of course, the last time he'd called Tanya, the woman from Hartworth he was sort of seeing, she didn't answer.

Figuring she'd slept in, Del tried again.

This time she answered.

"Rise and shine, sunshine," Del said. "I got up early for our day. Got permission for Richie to miss school, almost at his house, and then I'll get you and your boy."

"Del," she sounded frightened.

"What's wrong?"

"I don't know," she answered. "The police were by this morning. Hartworth's been shut down."

"What … what do you mean shut down?"

"Shut down. They said not to leave, that there's some horrible outbreak, and they're trying to keep us safe."

Del turned off the music completely. "I didn't hear anything about an outbreak, but I didn't watch the news."

"Well, I can tell you right now, I'm looking at a flier they dropped off at my door. They got the whole town closed down. Del … I'm scared. Mary from the store tried to go to work, and they sent her home. All stores are closed. She said she tried to leave town twice and couldn't get out. Sheriff, some deputies, all blocking the roads."

"Did she say if she saw signs of the government, military, men in those bio hazard suits?"

"I asked; she said no. Del …. I don't think the outbreak is outside of Hartworth."

"What do you mean?" Del asked.

"It's here in town. They ain't saying, but I can see from my apartment window. People are heading into the fire station, they look sick. Del … me and my boy aren't sick."

"Can you get out?"

"No. Can … you help?"

"What do you need me to do?"

"I don't care about me, but my son is only fourteen. Get him out of town. Please, come get him."

Del thought a moment. "Listen, I am almost at my ex's house. A minute away. Let me check the television, go online, see if I see anything. I'll ask her, she's one of those apocalypse nuts. If anyone knows anything, it's her."

"What about my son?"

"Dress him warm. Both of you, head out the back of the apartment, cross through the properties, and make your way toward Bailey's Ranch. Hit Bailey's dirt road that runs next to his property and through the hollow. It crosses the wooded area and meets Forty about two miles before town. Wait there. I'll get you."

"Are you sure?"

"Positive. Give me an hour," Del said.

"Thank you. I'll call you if there's a problem."

"Please do. Hang tight." Del ended the call just as he pulled into Emma's driveway. He saw Andy's truck. "Does that man *ever* work? Jeez."

◇◇◇◇

When Emma woke, she was surprised to find she was alone in bed. Cody wasn't there. Andy had stayed the night, as well. They were nowhere to be seen. She peeked at the time of nearly seven AM and knew that Richie was supposed to be up and ready to go with his father.

The smell of bacon and coffee told her all was well in Emma land, so she dressed then headed to the kitchen.

Cody was happily diving into a bowl of cereal, balancing on her knees, while Richie was half way through his plate.

"Morning," Emma said with a kiss to Andy's cheek as he stood at the stove. "This is nice."

"Th .. thought I'd c … cook before w … work. Eggs?"

"No," Emma answered. "Coffee is fine right now." She poured a cup and walked to the table. "Hey." She tapped Richie to get his attention. "Your dad is going to be here soon."

"I know. I know," he replied. "I'm ready. Just have to finish eating."

As she brought her mug to her lips, taking in that first sip of brew, the back door opened with a rush. Emma nearly choked when Del flew in. "You're not late; why are you rushing?" she asked.

"Have you watched TV at all? Been on the net?"

"No, I just woke up," she replied. "Andy?"

Andy shook his head and waved out for Richie. "You been online?"

Richie lifted his phone with a nod.

"What's up?" Emma asked.

"Something is happening," Del said. "I just talked to Tanya. Hartworth is quarantined. Shut down. They told her it's something outside of Hartworth, but she thinks it's inside."

"Oh my God. Hopefully Heather isn't back." She signed to Richie. "Can you check your phone see if there is any mention of a quarantine in Hartworth or even any friends online who may post that?" She turned to Del. "It has to be a mistake. I mean, about an outbreak outside of Hartworth. My alerts didn't sound off. It's gotta be in the town."

"That's what Tanya thinks," Del replied. "She wants me to get her kid out of town. I told her to send him past Bailey's Ranch."

"Del," Emma spoke seriously. "You can't do that."

"Why?" he asked.

"Because if the town is shut down and they have something, taking him out will break the barriers. It could spread the virus or whatever it is."

"He's not sick."

"But he may still be contagious."

"What do I do?" Del asked. "Seriously? If it were you, what would you want me to do? If you and Richie were stuck here?"

Emma thought about it. "Ok, I'd want Richie out, but I'd see how long the shutdown is; that tells the incubation period. Pull the kid, but keep him away for a day or two to make sure he doesn't get sick. If he doesn't, then it's fine. Wait it out somewhere."

"Bailey still park that RV near his property?" Del asked.

"Yep, he still shows his horses."

"We'll wait it out there." Del nodded. "Do you have a gun?"

Emma laughed. "Really?"

"You don't?"

Emma laughed again. "Really? You're asking me? I do; they're locked up. It's against the law to give you one. It isn't the end of the world, ya know, just a crazy coot sheriff flaunting his power." She looked at Andy.

"G .... G ... give him one." Then he held up two fingers twice.

"I'll give him a .22." Emma said. "Del, put on the TV, check to see if anything is on the news, and see if Richie found anything." She walked to the basement door. "And really, Del, I have to say this is pretty unselfish of you. I'm gonna make you a survival pack. Be right back."

"Do I need one? Can't I just bring a few cans?" Del asked.

"You need some water and food, and you need a lightweight pack in case you have to run. Breaking that kid out of quarantine is a crime. I'll make you a pack." She opened the basement door and disappeared for a few minutes. When she returned she carried what looked like a weight-loss belt and a small water camel.

She laid it flat on the table. "You have jerky, a small first aid pack, protein bars, and other things. It goes around your waist with Velcro, and strap this water over your shoulder. Keep it under your coat. It's designed to be hidden so people don't know what you have."

"Wow." Del blinked as he slipped it on under his coat and around his waist. "Where did you get this?"

"I made it. It's patented, so don't try to steal the idea."

"No, I'm not. You should let me invest in this." He secured it and closed his coat. "This is awesome."

Emma shrugged. 'We'll talk. Just …" She turned when the kitchen door opened again. "Dad?"

"What motel did Heather stay at last night?" Stew asked calmly, yet with concern.

"Brightside. Why?" Emma said. "I hate that place. Bunch of drunken truckers …" she slowed down her words when Stew walked to the television and turned it on.

"It burnt down last night," Stew said.

Emma gasped. "Oh my God." Immediately she sunk into a chair. Her insides fell to the floor. Her head spun trying to make heads or tails out of what she was feeling and feared. "She hasn't called."

"I know," Stew said. "I'm heading there now to see what I can find out."

"I'll come with you." Emma stood and turned to Andy. "Any way you can watch Cody?"

Richie interjected. "I'm here. Go. Please."

"G … G ..good luck," Andy told her.

"Thank you. I'll get my coat." She flew into the other room.

Del shook his head. "This is the oddest day. First Hartworth …"

"What happened in Hartworth?" Stew asked.

"Shut down," Del replied. "Quarantined. Nothing is on the news, but the sheriff closed it down."

"What the hell is the matter with Larry? He did this a few years back with the swine flu, remember?" Stew shook his head. "Said he was keeping it out, read about the idea in a book. He's insane. State Police will probably pacify him until tomorrow and force him to open back up again."

"Ready." Emma returned; she passed kisses to Andy, Richie, and Cody, then grabbed her purse. No sooner did she reach for her phone on the counter, it rang. Her eyes lifted. "Heather." It's Heather. Why is she face to facing me." Emma pressed 'accept' and waited for the connection.

"Maybe she can't get a phone signal, and internet access is all she has?" Stew suggested.

Emma nodded and then saw the word 'connected'; she was about to blurt out, 'Honey, are you okay?' but didn't the moment Heather's face showed in the video to video call. She was pale, gray pale, with what looked like a large black patch across the right side of her face extending down to her neck. She would have thought

Heather was burned, but her eyes were dark; the whites of her eyes were too dark. "Heather?"

"Mommy," Heather whimpered. "Mommy, I'm so sick. I don't know what's happening."

Emma closed her eyes for a moment and pulled the phone away from Cody's reach.

Cody called out 'Mamma' and Heather released a sob.

"Where are you?" Emma asked.

Stew peeked over her shoulder. "Baby, where are you?"

"At Roman's. I would have called, but I wanted you to see. Look at me. Something is wrong. The whole town is shut down, and I'm scared. I wanna come home. I just wanna come home. Val said I can't. He said a few days. Mommy … I think I'm dying."

The phone nearly dropped from Emma's hand. "Oh, sweetie. Oh, God, we'll get you help."

"Honey," Stew said. "I'm on my way."

Del added. "Me, too."

"Hurry," Heather cried. "Please. Mommy, Pap, I love you."

"I love you, baby," Emma said.

"Tell my baby I love her."

"She loves you." Emma tried to be strong.

"I'm on my way," Stew repeated. "Hang tight."

The call ended.

Emma immediately dropped her head to the phone and wept.

"Now we know why we haven't heard from her," Stew said.

Emma took a breath. "Ok, how do we do this? Larry has the town shut down."

"You and me," Stew said. "Don't do anything. Me and him …" He pointed to Del. "will."

"No." Emma shook her head. "I'm going."

"No, you aren't." Stew stepped forward, placing his hands firmly on her shoulders. "Did you look at Heather? Something is wrong."

"I know. That's why I am going. She's my daughter."

"And he is your son." Stew pointed to Richie. "And you have Cody here. What if Hartworth is shut down because everyone has what Heather has? What if the shutdown is real?"

"Tanya thinks so," Del added. "She believes the town is sick."

Stew nodded. "Then there you have it. I'll go and figure a way to get her out. At the very least she'll have someone there with her. If the town is sick, then I don't care if I get exposed. I care if you do." Stew kissed Emma on the forehead. "Del will be my diversion so I can sneak in. I think I know where Larry will have weak points. Ready?" he asked Del.

Del nodded. "I'll call you, Emma, as soon as your dad gets in." He walked to the door.

Stew stepped back. "Stay put, Emma. I mean it. I mean it. Andy, don't let her do anything stupid."

Andy held up his hand. "I … I promise."

Stew, with a solemn look, closed his mouth tightly and walked out of the house.

The moment the door closed, Emma turned to Andy. “My daughter.” Andy wrapped his arms around her, and she sunk into his arms.

Richie kept looking on his phone, telling Emma nothing was on the news or on the internet. That Heather would be fine, it couldn’t be that bad if it wasn’t on the news. But Emma didn’t believe that, not for one second. She had never seen an illness like the one that ravaged Heather. It scared her. The thought that the sickness was so bad that they didn’t just want it out of Hartworth, they didn’t want news of it out, scared her even more.

FLASH FORWARD

Ground Zero – 7

December 23rd

Hartworth, Montana

December 17th, 10:05 p.m. – It is worse than I had feared. The radius of exposure goes further and, I believe, encompasses the whole town. The further away from ground zero, the less exposure, the more time for symptoms. Thankfully, the amount of germ released wasn't enough to filter into a neighboring town. After eight hours, it dissipated. We have taken all that we could into the fire hall. Volunteers are now falling ill, but still strong enough to help. Anyone else infected has been turned away and remain in their homes. Many have gone to the borders and were turned away. Seeking help at a nearby hospital. Fools. Do they not know the death sentence they could deliver. Are they that selfish that they don't care who they infect? They need only to look around them. While I understand they are concerned for themselves, at this late point, they need to concern themselves with humanity. Mankind's survival, for their survival is lost. By tomorrow at this time, no one will be well enough to help out or seek help.. It is my guess that the wave of death will begin in twenty-four hours. There will be some that will not succumb, but they will not be the same. Not only will they be physically scarred, but hunted down by anyone who finds this town in the days following its demise. I am still in debate as to what should be done with that fraction.

Edward shook his head. ‘Well, the bodies with bullet holes tells us what he did with that fraction.”

“It wasn’t an execution,” Harold said. “I think these people were shot in their homes or on the street and brought to that garage. Eighty-three, to be exact. Maybe they planned on burning the garage.”

“Maybe,” Edward said. “We’ve accounted for three hundred people so far. Still a lot more to go.”

“Impossible task to handle until we get help. There’s only four of us.”

Edward looked at his watch. “The first wave should be landing in Billings now. They’ll be here soon.” His head jolted at the sound of the phone, and he leaned to retrieve it. “Yes.”

He listened and shifted his eyes to Harold.

“That’s not possible,” Edward said. “Are we sure? I’ll wait. Thank you.” He hung up.

“What is it?” Harold asked.

“They think they know what it is. That was the main lab. They are checking again, but they are ninety percent sure they identified it.”

"How can they identify something like this?" Harold asked. "We've been doing this a long time, and I've never seen anything like it."

"Yes, we have, if you think about it." Edward turned and brought the image of the virus onto the screen. "Look at it. It makes sense."

"Well, I don't know what you're talking about," Harold said. "It's a mutation. Maybe two viruses mutated together."

"You're right," Edward told him.

"I'm right? We've been saying since we looked at it that it was a mutation of two viruses."

"But it's not a natural mutation, it is a deliberate combination of two viruses."

"I'm … I'm sorry?" Harold said, stunned and a little lost.

Edward pointed to the virus structure as he explained. "We have been at this a long time, but we didn't recognize it because we aren't old enough. It's a Cold War creation, one we thought was a myth. One never really proven other than on paper and in reports."

"Oh my God." Harold stumbled back. "I see it. I see the two. Holy shit. That isn't the tail sequence to any hemorrhagic fever. That's Ebola."

"And that …" Edward indicted. "Is smallpox. This is what Ebolapox looks like under the microscope. Out there is what it looks like when it hits."

"Jesus Christ. The communicability rate and infectious level of smallpox combined with the lethality and brutality of Ebola." He swiped his hand down his face.

"Yeah, well, they need only to look at this town to see someone didn't just create a damn deadly virus," Edward said. "They created mankind's extinction nightmare."

Chapter Nine

Hartworth, Montana

December 17th

Vivian knew it wasn't just a bad cold or a case of the flu when she peered into the toilet bowl and saw the remnants of her regurgitation. It was black, thick, foul smelling and didn't even resemble vomit. It looked more like tar. The vomiting hit her like nothing she had ever experienced. Unlike any stomach bug or case of food poisoning, this wasn't a wave of extreme nausea. There was a slight twist that happened in her gut and, involuntarily, the substance made its way up her esophagus before she even realized it was happening.

She had no control. It shot out of her mouth and through her fingertips before she even made it to the bathroom. No holding it back.

Perhaps her body did give signs that it was happening, but she was far too weak to know it.

Vivian told Doc that she'd head to the fire hall for treatment in the makeshift hospital. But she grew weaker, and then the vomiting started. She didn't make it. She feared her children would come down with whatever she had.

Weakened, she sat on the floor by the commode, unable to stand, not only staring at what came from her mouth, but sitting in a puddle of diarrhea that flowed from her. She couldn't move; her arms ached and burned. A black patch started on her hands and forearms. Vivian couldn't even manage to go back to bed.

She tried to call for help, but no one came. No one showed up, not her husband or her children.

All she could do was stay there, struggling not to vomit and crying in between each straining gag.

◇◇◇◇

About three quarters of a mile away, just past the road to Bailey's Ranch, Stew had Del pull over so he could get a look.

Sure enough, like he suspected, the road block was just outside of town. The sheriff's car and a pickup truck were parked sideways on the road.

"Ok, pull back on the road." Stew put down the binoculars. "I'm getting out here and cutting across the Doyle property. There's a road that leads into town. Keep your phone on; I'll be listening. If they let you in through the barricade, I wanna hear, and I'll meet you at Doc Paltrov's place."

Del nodded. "I understand. They aren't gonna let me through."

"Probably not. Keep the phone on," Stew instructed. "Keep them talking so they don't see me.

The property starts to run perpendicular to where the roadblock is. I need you to be a diversion."

"Got it."

"Go to the RV, meet that boy. You sent that text, right?"

"I did. I'll meet him there then I'll call my manager once I'm safe and get word out."

"That's the plan." Stew opened the truck door. "Good luck."

"Get my daughter, Stew."

"I don't know what will happen. But I will do my damnedest to get to her and, hopefully, get her home."

Another nod from Del, and Stew stepped out of the truck.

He quietly shut the door and hurried off the side of the road onto the Doyle property. He checked the phone; his call to Del was still connected. He kept it to his ear as he walked, wanting to hear everything that went on. But that didn't last long; merely a few feet into his journey, the shifting of a shotgun chamber caught Stew's attention. As he lifted his hands, his thumb accidentally pressed the 'end' button.

"Where you headed, Stew?" Doyle stood there.

"Look, Doyle …" Stew lowered his hands. "I'm not here to cause harm. I'm heading into town."

"I can't let you do that. I promised the sheriff I'd keep an eye out."

"I understand that and appreciate that. I also know that you've been told that people are sick outside of Hartworth. That's not true. I promise you with everything I am, I am not sick. I'm a man of my word, Doyle, you know that."

"I do," Doyle nodded. "And Stew, you have a family, that's why I can't let you go into town. It's bad, Stew. Some sort of flu got a grip on things. It's bad. I seen it."

"I did, too." Stew said. "When my granddaughter called using the video phone. She's sick. She's really sick. Like I have never seen. She's alone in there, Doyle, I have to get to her."

"It's bad, Stew," Doyle reiterated.

"I don't care if I don't ever leave, but I have to get to her. I have to."

Finally Doyle lowered his gun, and with a wave of his weapon, he summoned Stew to follow. "Let's go."

"Where to?"

"Too long of a walk. I'll drive you. My truck's over there."

"Thank you. Thank you very much." As Stew followed, he looked down at his phone; the call was disconnected. He wasn't worried too much about it, he made it. He was certain Del would be just fine.

◇◇◇◇

"Mr. Del Ray Lewis, ain't that what you call yourself now, Mr. Rock Star?" Larry stepped around his sheriff's car. "Hands in the air. What do you got?"

"Just my phone." Del lifted his hands. "I need to get into town."

"No can do. Guess you haven't watched the news. There's a sickness going on, and I shut my town down to keep it safe."

"Sheriff, I saw the news, there's no sickness." Del kept his distance. "I also talked to my daughter. She's in there. She's sick. I need to get to her."

"Very nice of you to show some concern for your child. But I can't let you in. Turn around. Come back in a couple days."

Del laughed. "Seriously? You can't do this. State Police …."

"Have already said do what I need to do." Larry smiled.

"Yeah, well, my gut is saying that I am gonna do what I need to do," Del said as he took a step back toward his truck. "Something is happening in that town. Something bad that you don't want anyone to know about. What did you call me? Mr. Rock Star. Check this out, Sheriff. You need help shutting down this town. One call …" Del showed his phone. "This rock star is letting the news break."

Larry raised his weapon. "You can't do that, Del. Give it a day."

"Sorry."

"Del, I am telling to you to not get in the truck. To stop right now."

Del reached for the truck door.

"Del, last warning. Stop or I'll shoot."

Del laughed as he turned and faced Larry. "Shoot? Seriously? What the hell are you trying to keep in there? What did you do? Unreal." Del shook his head and reached out for his driver's door. "You aren't shooting me."

Bang.

Larry didn't want to shoot Del; it was the last thing he wanted to do. He could still see Del take that shot, square in the belly, and fly back into the truck. It made him sick to think of what he did, but he didn't have a choice. He didn't.

One call, one post on the internet, and it was over. Authorities would flock into town. Unable to save the day, they'd know right away it was a biological weapon. With Larry unaffected, he'd go down. Larry worked too hard his whole life to be the good guy to spend the rest of his days in prison for killing a town. Keeping it quiet meant also keeping the bug in the town.

One man's life was an even trade. In a couple days time it wouldn't matter. The bug would have run its course and Larry would be long gone.

He drove Del's truck into town with Del in the back. He was still alive; Larry heard him moan, but he knew he wouldn't be alive for long.

"You shot him, Sheriff. You shot him." Bret, the local man on the road block, said.

"I know. I know." Larry took a moment to think. "I'll take him into town for help. He's not bleeding that bad. Doc's there."

Larry drove off. He had no intention of seeking help for Del. None whatsoever. But he had to do something with him, he couldn't' leave him on the side of the road, nor could he let it get out that he shot the big superstar Del Ray Lewis.

A few days, two tops, Larry figured was all he needed to keep the Del shooting a secret. The town was wrapped up in the sickness. Already a quarter of the people were ill. Folks were consumed with staying inside, safe, and observing the quarantine. No one should notice, and no one did.

Larry pulled the pickup to the back of the police station. Del wasn't a big man, and Larry was strong enough to carry him alone.

He brought him in the back door then immediately down to the basement where the holding cells were located. With a whispered apology, he set Del inside a cell, then shut and locked the door.

No one would know, no one would look, and after checking out Del's lifeless body one more time, Larry went about his business. He would do what he needed to do to keep everything quiet and to keep the sickness from getting out of Hartworth.

Del was proof of that.

◇◇◇◇

Val and his band of merry door knockers weren't even halfway through the town, and already he had changed the plan from telling people to come to the fire hall to stay in their homes.

He promised help to those who reported sickness. For appearances,Val wrote down their names and house numbers knowing full well he'd never be back. He couldn't.

He was optimistic in believing that the fire hall would hold enough.

A simple sign on the door made it a makeshift clinic, but it was nothing more than a mere waiting bay of death.

Here were volunteers to give aspirin and morphine, wipe faces, but those who stayed at home at least suffered in privacy.

There was no privacy, no dignity at the fire hall. People vomited everywhere. The moans overcame the echoing hall like a bad music system playing over an intercom.

It looked and smelled of sheer death.

How many times did Val say, "This is just the worst before it gets better. You'll be fine, in a couple days you'll forget about how sick you feel. It'll be fine."

Val knew better. Already, their eyes were darkening, skin had turned gray, and many were already scratching themselves until they bled.

He was tired and worried about his son. He hadn't been home in two hours, and it was time to return.

Eighteen people volunteered to help, and Val could hear them sniffle and cough.

It wouldn't be long before *they* left, and those who remained, those who suffered on blankets and cots, vomiting into plastic grocery store bags, would be alone.

Something needed to be done.

Val would think about that, but until he came up with a solution to the people in the fire hall, he had to check on his son and Heather.

Exhausted, Val stepped from the fire hall, walking by the long line of people.

"Doctor, I'm sick,"

"Help me."

"What's going on?"

Val kept walking; he couldn't look at any of them. He kept his eyes straight ahead. Had he not, he wouldn't have seen Stew Burton in the passenger's seat of Doyle's truck.

Stew was in town. Val's heart dropped. He knew where Stew was headed, and Val picked up his pace.

<><><><>

"Heather!" Stew called out as he entered Val's home. It wasn't easy; the doors were locked and Stew ended up breaking the glass to get inside.

He immediately headed to the staircase that led to the home upstairs.

"Heather." He charged to the second floor. No one was in the living room, and no one answered his call. There was a hall that Stew could only assume led to the bedroom. Still calling he looked in the first room. Empty. At the second door, mid-call, Stew stopped. There were twin beds in that room and clearly someone lay on one of them. Stew walked to the first bed. "Heather." He whispered and pulled down the covers some.

"Dear God," he gasped. Immediately Stew felt sick. It wasn't Heather; it was Roman. Non-responsive, wheezing with each breath, shivering. His skin was black as if it were charcoal. A slight moan seeped from Roman, and Stew lifted the covers back over him. He spun from the room, calling out, and stopped when he heard what sounded like a cat's growl.

It came from the next room, and as soon as Stew reached for the door he saw feet.

Calling out her name, he opened the door to see Heather lying on the bathroom floor.

She was surrounded by a pool of a thick dark substance, and her hand reached for the commode. Turning her head, she eyes locked with Stew. "Pap. Help."

"Oh my God, baby." He crouched down to her. "Oh my God." Stew's heart broke, it literally broke as he reached for her. The moment he touched her, she cried out. It wasn't loud, but it was shrill. Obviously, her skin, black to the sight, was agonizing to her.

"I have to get you out of here. I have to get you help." He stood, ran out to the first bedroom, ripped the comforter from the bed, and brought it to the bathroom. Gently he placed it over Heather. "I know this is going to hurt, but I have to get you out. Okay?"

Heather nodded.

As best he could, as careful as he could, using the comforter as a cushion, Stew lifted Heather into his arms. She whimpered as her head fell to his chest.

He had done it.

Stew managed to carry her down the hall and the stairs. He was almost to the door when Val called out.

"Stop, Stew. I cannot let you take her," Val said calmly.

"Are you insane?" Stew asked as he turned around, ready to blast him, but didn't because Val extended a revolver. "You are."

Val shook his head. "She has to stay here."

"Over my dead body."

"It's already dead, Stew, you just don't know it yet. You're not indestructible. This virus is. Put her back in bed, let me give her another dose of morphine. She'll rest," Val said.

"She needs to go to a hospital. You hear me?" Stew's voice rose with emotion. "She needs help."

"They can't help her. Look at her. She's got another day, day and a half. Tops."

"I have to try."

"Start by putting her down; every second you hold her is a second of pain that girl feels. She can't express it. But she feels it, knows it."

"Listen to me," Stew said. "I'm turning around and getting her help."

"Then I'll shoot you both," Val said. "Although shooting Heather might be the humane thing to do."

"You're sick."

"Unfortunately, I'm not. Take her back up, Stew. I've killed already to keep this virus contained, I won't stop with you."

In defeat, Stew lowered his head and walked by Val to the stairs. He carried Heather up and took her to the empty bedroom, laying her on the large bed.

"I'm sorry, sweetheart." Stew adjusted the covers and pillows, trying to make her comfortable. "I tried. I'll figure something out. Until then, I won't leave your side." He leaned down and kissed her. His lips tightened and a lump formed in his throat as he choked on his own emotions.

"I am sorry to be so harsh," Val stated as he walked into the room. "I have to be." He walked to the bed.

"Your son … your own son," Stew said, "is sick. Dying. Don't you want to help him?"

"I do. It is beyond us now. That is why we have to stay here. Keep them here. Keep … you here now." Val pulled down some of the covers on Heather and lifted a syringe. "This will keep her comfortable. This is very contagious. As much as I worry about them, there are others we have to worry about. Others outside this town. Your child. Our grandchildren."

Stew gasped. "Val, listen, there are people who are experienced in sickness like this. They know what they're doing."

"So do I," Val replied. "More than you realize. I also know this virus more than anyone."

"What are you talking about?"

"I worked on it, I helped shape it."

Stew stood. "You son of a bitch. You did this. My daughter was right."

"Yes. She was, in a sense." Val tossed the empty syringe. "When she started producing pictures, I had to commit her to silence her and so no one would take her seriously. "

Stew lowered back to the bed. "I bought it. Had I not, this wouldn't have happened."

"Oh, it would have happened," Val said. "Maybe not now, but exposing me meant either the virus was unattended or handed over. Turning the virus over would set off a time bomb."

"The bomb went off!" Stew yelled. "Look at this town. Look at these kids."

"It went off here. Here. Sealed in," Val stated firmly. "We have a shot at containing this. We take this virus, one patient, beyond the barriers of this town, and we can forget it, because it will spread like wildfire. We have to keep this thing tight. Keep it here. If we don't, who knows. It's the end for the state. They will have no choice but to burn out Montana." Val walked to the door. "God help them if they don't."

FLASH FORWARD

Ground Zero – 8

December 23rd

Hartworth, Montana

The last thing Edward wanted to do was suit up and walk to the fire hall. He understood that his four-person team was ambitious and wanted to have answers, but help was on the way, and the entire vision of the town bothered Edward like nothing else.

It was as if he were previewing an apocalypse he'd rather not face.

He liked the mobile lab; it was warm in there, secluded, and he couldn't see outside. Couldn't see the horrors. A dead town, sucked of life in every way imaginable.

But Martha and Goldman were convinced there were a lot of answers, not just bodies in the fire hall. After all that's where they found the journal.

The journal.

Edward was nearly done. He wanted to finish reading it before the backup teams arrived. He had just gotten off the phone with the CDC.

"Even though it may have died here," Edward told them, "a health bulletin, especially in this area, needs to be issued. ER doctors and PCPs are going to dismiss it as the everyday flu. Contact victims were exhibiting flu-like symptoms twenty-four hours after exposure. It took another day for full-blown effects to start to hit, unlike our ground zero victims where the virus raged through them at an astronomical rate."

"We'll issue the bulletin," the director said. "But it's the 23rd. That town was dead by the 20th or 21st. If there were contact victims, if they broke the barrier, they had full-blown symptoms in twenty-four hours. Come on, Edward. A contact victim outside of Hartworth would be dead by now. Surely, we would have heard of a case of a person's skin turning black, throwing up blood."

"That's initial contact victims. We don't know how long the virus takes when a contact victim passes it along. Plus, I'm basing this info on the town. Even the contact victims could have had ground zero exposure. We don't know. We can't tell who is who yet. Right now we need to be diligent. This is so frightening that we need to scare people about it."

"We are working on that. We need to understand it before we inform the general public."

"How can we understand something that was considered a 'paper project' only?" Edward asked.

"There was a similar outbreak in Pakistan in 2002. Small town. Very similar. It didn't break boundaries because it killed its host too fast."

"Let's hope that is the case," Edward said. He ended the call without a single optimistic feeling in his body. That was when he got the call to suit up and head to the fire hall.

He tromped through the fresh snow to the fire hall. The door was open.

Martha was in there alone; Harold had joined Goldman on a venture. They had managed to cover the bodies and record them.

"What's up, Martha?" Edward asked.

"Two things," Martha said with a wave of her hand. "One, that body of Vivian Morris. She didn't die here."

Edward cocked back. "We got her from here."

"She didn't die here. We removed her and the others from here because they were nearest to the door. I think they were brought in. Someone made an attempt to tag everyone, sick and dead."

"Ok, so, what made you come up with this determination?"

"Because the more I examined the bodies further in, the more I noticed the difference. The ones by the door looked like Vivian Morris. These …" She uncovered a body. "Look slightly different."

Edward tossed up his hands. He looked at the body of the young man; most of his body was black, his mouth agape and head turned to the left, a pool of regurgitation next to him. "What's different?"

"Look at the lips. The fingertips on his left hand. The hand that isn't black."

Edward examined the hand and the lips. "They're blue. Cold?"

"Nope. Carbon monoxide levels are through the roof. Unlike Vivian, most of these people died of carbon monoxide poisoning."

"What the hell?"

"Mercy killing, nearest I can figure. How do you mercifully put two hundred people out of their misery? Just like this. Somebody started the cleanup of the town, hence why all the houses around the hall were empty. And all the bodies near the door were just laid there. Vivian's name isn't on the fire hall list. She came in after. Brought here for discovery. Whoever did it, I think, just gave up, it was too much, too many. I really think the cleanup was after these people were put out of their misery."

"How did you discover all this?"

"I was cross-checking the names on the town census against the fire hall registration list. I thought it was odd that Vivian wasn't on there. Then I noticed Bill Smith's lips. For the hell of it, I did a reading. Ventilation was shut down, Kerosene heaters were used along with the buildings' own heating system that was rigged. But I can only guess that was the source. That's not my forte. But let me show you something else. Follow me."

What else could there be, Edward wondered. Apparently his team was right in assuming the fire hall was a gold mine of information. It made sense. They opened it up as a aid station. There was no way to help them, they were suffering, so someone killed them. Was it the same someone who decided to organize the dead, make sure Edward's job of identifying bodies would be a little easier?

Martha led Edward to the kitchen of the fire hall and to a storage closet. "Bingo supplies. And I got a bingo." She opened the door.

"Jesus," Edward blurted out when she saw the body of a man sitting in a chair, his lips and hands blue. A white substance rolled from his mouth. The most foretelling was the white piece of paper pinned to his chest, a suicide note that simply read, 'Forgive me, Hartworth.' "No outward signs of the virus. Our Carbon Bomber?" Edward asked.

"I doubt it, unless he wore oxygen until he was ready to die. Whoever killed the fire hall people carried bodies in. I saw no signs of oxygen. He could have been the one. We don't know. But we do know who he is." She moved the note slightly to expose a name tag. "Larry Meadows, town sheriff."

"Explains how they easily shut down the town." Just as Edward closed his eyes to take it all in, Harold burst into the room.

"Whoa, who's that?" Harold asked.

"Town sheriff," Martha answered.

"Oh, yeah?" Harold said. "Come with me. I just found the town doctor."

Chapter Ten

Lincoln, Montana

December 18th

Andy had barely slept. In fact, he estimated it was just before dawn when he fell asleep in the chair next to Emma's bed. It was a long day and night. He hadn't left her side, nor even gone into town.

He couldn't leave her, not in the state Emma was in. Typically, she was optimistic, bubbly, but the day before Emma was devastated. So much to the point, she couldn't even care for Cody. Couldn't look at her granddaughter without bursting into tears.

Richie was just as bad.

The video call from Heather started a chain reaction of heartbreak. When Stew and Del left, Emma paced. She heard nothing from either of them for the longest time. Then Stew called. It was the beginning of the end of Emma's world.

Emma placed the call on speaker so Andy could interpret for Richie. He stammered as much in signing as he did in talking over the conversation.

"I'm with her," Stew told Emma. "Sweetheart, it's not good."

"Can't you get her to a hospital in Billings?"

"She can't be moved, Emma, and she can't be helped."

Emma sobbed; her shoulders dropped. "Can you bring her home?"

"I can't do that. This thing … is bad, Emma. Chances are, I'm gonna be sick, too. Something was released here, something horrendous. State Police know the town is shut down, and I really think today, maybe tomorrow, health officials will be swarming. Until then I can't leave. I can't take that chance with you or Richie or the baby or anyone outside this town. Understand?"

"How many people are sick?"

"Hundreds, and they're expecting the whole town to get it. This thing ripped through. Do not … do not leave the house. Do not attempt to come here. I know you."

"I need to see my daughter. I need to tell her I love her. I need to hold her."

"You can't," Stew replied. "When she wakes, she'll call."

"I need to hold her. She needs her mother."

"Yes, yes, she does. But she also needs her mother healthy for her own child. Think about this, Emma," Stew spoke strongly. "Reverse it. If this was you, if you were sick, would you want me near you, or would you want me to take care of your child?"

Emma swiped her hand hard across her cheek. "There's gotta be a way for me to get close without catching this."

"Maybe once health officials get here, but not now."

"What if they don't come?" Emma asked.

"Then we'll figure out something. Emma …" Stew paused. "Please, as much as this is breaking my heart, our girl isn't making it. I have never seen anyone so sick in my life."

"Is she in pain, Dad?"

"No. Not right now. I'm gonna go. I'll call you back."

Emma looked at Richie who tapped her arm and asked a question. She relayed it to Stew. "Daddy, have you spoken to Del? We can't get through to him."

"He was fine when I left. Probably at the RV now."

Emma accepted that, conveyed her love, and ended the call. Then Emma collapsed into a fit of crying, holding on to Cody, a child who was just so confused about what was going on.

She hyperventilated as she breathed and intermittently burst out with a scream of sorrow.

"I can't do this, Andy. I can't," Emma cried. "I'm losing my daughter. I can't live through this. I can't do this."

"You … have to." Andy told her. "I know it's h … hard. You have to. You … you will." That was all Andy could tell her. What else can you say to a woman whose child is dying?

Richie wasn't as sad at first. He was angry. "How can you just sit there?" he asked Emma. "How can you not want to go after her? This is my sister."

"And she is my daughter," Emma said. "I want to be there. But you tell me who will be there for Cody if we all get sick? Who?"

"So when did the baby become more important than your own child?"

"This is my daughter's child, and the baby is the most important thing in the world to her. Don't do this to me, Richie. Don't. Please don't," Emma begged.

It went back and forth, Richie's anger treading over Emma's guilt.

Andy tried to intervene and explain to Richie that his mother was going through as difficult a time as he was, that Emma didn't need to feel additional guilt. It escalated all night; each phone call from Stew or conversation with Heather caused another. Each futile attempt to reach Del caused anguish and frustration. All Andy could do was be there for her.

Finally, the fighting ceased. It went from arguing to sharing sadness just before everyone grew tired. There was no resolution to anything, and Andy knew that caused more frustration. Heather was dying, and Emma couldn't see or hold her daughter. Richie couldn't see his sister or speak to his father.

Things hung on a cliff.

Andy said his goodnight to Richie and promised him the next morning they'd work on a plan, a plan to solve things. He watched the boy try one more time to text his father, but there was no response. Then Andy held Cody while Emma curled up beside him. When both Cody and Emma were sound asleep, Andy slipped from bed, cleaned the house, and went on the internet.

He posted on a social media site and sent an email to a news station asking if they were aware of a quarantine in the town of Hartworth.

Andy hoped for the best from his attempts but didn't expect much. After that, he read a while and fell asleep in the recliner next to Emma's bed.

He woke up before Emma and Cody; they were both sound asleep. Figuring it best not to wake them, Andy went to the kitchen and made coffee. The house was quiet and calm, and wanting to keep his promise to Richie, Andy went to his bedroom.

It would be the perfect time to talk to him.

Outside of Richie's bedroom was a light switch, the equivalent to a knock. Andy flipped the switch a few times then opened the door.

Richie's bed was not only made, it was empty. Immediately Andy panicked. Where was Richie? Before he woke Emma, Andy sought his phone. He would text Richie; try to get in touch with him.

Maybe he went to his grandfather's ranch or even into town.

Before Andy could even send a message to Richie, he saw that he had one from the teenager. Andy's fears were confirmed when he read the simple message: "Went to find Dad. We will get Heather.'

◇◇◇◇

It wasn't even eight in the morning, but Larry was downing his second shot of bourbon. Maybe because he hadn't been to bed he felt it was fine to replace his coffee with something a bit stronger and more calming.

He was exhausted; the day before was a day from hell. He could tell by the quiet of the street and lack of movement that this day would be better … he hoped.

He had just returned from the posts in town, replacing ill men with men not quite so sick. However, he knew Beck Harper wasn't far from turning.

Turning.

That's what Larry started calling it. Why Doc didn't put that in his little journal, Larry didn't know. He stole a peek of it when it was on the desk at the fire hall.

Those who were exposed initially took a one step at a time, one symptom at a time, route to the black sickness. However, those who caught it from the initial victims woke up feeling bad or started feeling it and jumped from an everyday common cold to near death, they didn't gradually feel worse. It was a flip of the switch. He learned that when his one guard started sneezing at two in the morning and by seven had to be removed. He was vomiting, unable to move, and his skin was turning black.

Larry shot him. In fact, Larry shot many people in the early morning hours, his way of saving them from what he witnessed at the fire hall.

The later victims, or contact victims, as Doc called them, probably got a mutated form. Viruses mutate to survive. Those contact victims were catching up to the exposed ones.

If Doc was keeping a journal for whoever found the town, he needed to make a note about the mutation.

At least, Larry thought that he should.

His last stop was the fire hall, and then Larry planned to rest for a few hours.

Doc was coming out of the hall, that journal tucked under his arm.

"How is it in there?" he asked Doc.

Doc shook his head. "Nothing that can be done. Tomorrow evening we will start to see the deaths. By the next day, the town."

Mouth closed tight, Larry nodded. "They're suffering pretty bad in there, Doc."

"Nothing I can do. There's not enough medication to ease them."

"Maybe … maybe you know we should have called for help," Larry suggested. "I know this is on us. But right now, I'm thinking I'd rather go down as a bad guy then watch these people suffer." He lowered his voice to a whisper. "We had over seventy calls to the emergency service office last night. We lied to these people about help coming. People ran to get out of town … they were stopped. By me." He spoke with choked up words. "I'm mercy killing, Doc. How wrong is that?"

"Your God will forgive you, if that's what you're worried about."

"My God?" Larry laughed. "I am not worried about burning in hell, 'cause if there is a hell, I already got a spot reserved. We should have called for help."

"Should have. Could have. It's too late. You bring people in here before this burns out and we open up the seal."

"How do we know it didn't escape?"

"I'm confident it didn't. But if it did, I am also confident that those who caught it are far too ill to get out of bed or call for help. It'll burn out before it spreads."

"So in the meantime, before the call for help is placed, we just let these people slowly suffer."

"What choice is there?" Doc asked. "A few shots of morphine and some comfort for these town folks are worth the chance of letting this out?" He shook his head. "No. We have no choice. No. Excuse me, I'll be back. I just have to check on my son."

Larry watched as Doc walked away. He looked back to the fire hall thinking, 'nothing can be done?' Larry couldn't accept that.

<><><><>

Lincoln, Montana

The gentle tap on her shoulder told Emma something wasn't right. She had hoped with all her might that when she woke, everything that happened the day before was nothing but a nightmare or a bad dream, but Andy's face told her that it wasn't.

Reality was about to blast her.

He set a cup of coffee on the nightstand, and after placing his fingers to his lips with a point to the baby, he waved for Emma to follow him.

Internal instincts told Emma to sip that coffee on the way to the kitchen. It was cold in the house, and the fresh blanket of snow outside sent in a gray look. It felt eerier.

Her stomach knotted in fear. "Please, Andy, tell me my daughter didn't die."

Andy shook his head. "No. But …" He lowered his head and handed her his phone. "Richie is g … gone. Le … left."

She stammered a questioning word, and then looked down at the message on the phone. "Oh my God." Emma whimpered. "He's exposing himself to find his father. Why would he do that?"

"No … no matter w ... what, it is his d-dad," Andy replied and grabbed his coat off the chair. "He … needs to f-feel chiv-chiv .." He twitched his head. "Chivalrous."

"I'll get the baby. We'll .."

"No," Andy said firmly.

"This is ridiculous, Andy. It is. I can't see my dying daughter. My son is out there. What kind of mother am I to stay put and do nothing but wait?"

"A g… good one. C-Cody needs you. Th … that is your priority."

"My children need me."

"Th..th…they are grown. Stay p-put."

"But, Andy, please. I can't do this. I don't care anymore. I don't. I'm losing my daughter; if I lose my son …"

"Cody."

Emma lowered her head. "I need you, too. I do. Andy … if you go, what if you get sick?"

"Better m .. me than you. I'll be … be .. careful. I promise." He pulled on his coat.

"This is insane." Emma dropped to a chair.

Andy held up a finger, walked into the next room, and returned with a book. He placed it on the table before her. It was one of the books he wrote. "It's smart." He tapped the cover then proceeded without a stutter to recite what he knew. "Entire communities and civilizations ceased to exist and were rendered extinct because they failed to use common sense. Lack of preparation, an emotional mistake …stupid avoidable errors. Stay put." Andy said. "That is smart. Not insane." He inched the book nearer to her. Then after kissing her on the cheek, Andy grabbed his phone and walked out.

<><><><>

Hartworth, Montana

It was the beginning of the end. Stew was well aware of the reality when he woke up.

He knew it would happen. How could it not? He held Heather, wiped her down, and stayed close, face-to-face. Every whimper she made he was there to comfort as best as he could. The only time he left her side was to go to the bathroom or look out the window.

Every car sound, motor sound, Stew looked with enthusiasm, hoping that it was the CDC or someone. However, they didn't show up, and as each hour passed less activity occurred outside the window.

He spent the evening watching his granddaughter. He prayed often, not for God to make her well, but to stop her suffering, and he thanked God. He thanked God for Heather.

Reflections of the past, of the first day he saw her and held her. How his heart opened up to a love he never thought he'd feel. He vowed she'd be special, and she was. He remembered her first day of school, taking her there and waiting outside.

How many school days did the sheriff come and ask him to leave, to stop stalking the school?

Heather was his precious gift from heaven. It broke his heart that she was suffering. The only saving grace was that Stew would not have to live long with the pain of losing her. He'd die knowing the joy of Heather rather than the grief of her loss.

The world of Hartworth grew increasingly quiet. Stew supposed people were too ill to care or to move. If there was an inkling of hope for help, it disappeared as the hours moved on.

Heather slept. Val had given her another shot. It calmed her as she convulsed. She was literally throwing up her insides. They broke down, bit by bit, and found their way out.

In that quiet moment, Stew took his opportunity. He lifted the phone, sniffled, and dialed. "Hey, there, Andy. It's Stew. Listen, I'm calling you because you need to know, and we need to come up with a plan. I'm not gonna make it either, Andy … I'm sick."

◇◇◇◇

Richie realized how insane it was to leave his home. He was driven by emotions and took his mother's car, even though he didn't have a license and didn't drive very well. He didn't think it through until he hit the main stretch of road just before Hartworth.

He just wanted to find his father. He didn't pass another car or even see another car until the roadblock was in sight. That's when he saw, just beyond the pickup truck, several dozen cars, just parked there.

Richie stopped way ahead of the roadblock. He wasn't getting through. He knew that. All he wanted to find out was if anyone had seen his father, but the reality of his handicap hit him the second he stepped from the car.

He could talk, but would they be able to understand him? Did they know sign language?

A few feet out of the car, a man with a shotgun staggered forward. He said something.

Richie held his hands to his ear and shouted, "I am deaf."

The man stepped closer. His mouth moved and then, horrifying Richie, he paused and vomit just shot from his mouth. It seemed to surprise the man as much as it did Richie.

The man buckled over and another raced forward.

Richie watched as the first man still vomited, seemingly out of control. Fearful of getting closer or that he already had gotten too close, Richie spun, jumped in the car, shut the door, and put it in reverse.

He sloppily turned around on the road, confident he could get away, and wondered instantly if he should even attempt to go back home. He made it only about a hundred feet when the car swerved viciously and out of control to the left, across the road, and off the grade.

Without wearing a seatbelt, Richie flew up, and his head bashed against the roof of the car. He then hit his forehead on the steering wheel, just before the airbags deployed and the car came to a complete halt.

Richie remained motionless on purpose for the longest time, just in case the men came for him. He locked the doors of the car and reached for the phone as slowly as he could.

<><><><>

Lincoln, Montana

Andy didn't want to take a chance on going through town. He hadn't received a single phone call about going to work, or rather about not showing up, and he didn't want to chance the Sheriff seeing him leave. He took the long way across Stew's property, going south and then coming up north. The roads were bad, even the main ones. Where were the state trucks?

Just as he hit the main route six miles outside of Lincoln, he got the call from Stew. That call made Andy stop.

He pulled over. He was too emotional to drive. Stew sounded horrible; Andy couldn't believe the turn of events. Three days earlier, they decorated the Christmas tree. He and Emma went toy shopping for Cody. Now, Christmas wasn't going to happen. It wasn't going to be the same … ever. How was he to tell Emma? It was all falling down. Heather was dying, her father was sick, her son missing, Del missing. The only redeeming feature was Cody. Was she enough to pull Emma through?

Andy talked to Stew for a while. They talked about many things, and then Andy took a few minutes after that call before he could think clearly enough to drive.

He had just put the truck in drive when his phone beeped.

Richie sent a text.

'Help me. I don't know what to do. I'm scared.'

◇◇◇◇

Hartworth, Montana

There was something about Andy. Richie had known him his entire life, but over the last few weeks as his mother and Andy became a real couple, that was when he realized the value of Andy. He was a good guy, and he gave him a sense of security.

Andy was also the only person Richie could think of to text; just communicating with him made everything seem like it would be all right.

'Help me. I don't know what to do. I'm scared,' texted Richie.

'Where are you?'

'Just outside of Hartworth.'

"On my way.'

'Don't come,' Richie told him. 'I'm scared. They shot mom's car. I'm on the side of the road. I think I got too close.'

'Are they near you now?' Andy asked.

'No. They are sick. Real sick. I think I got too close. What do I do? This is real.'

'Are you hurt?'

'No. What do I do? I don't want to get sick. But if I got it, I can't go near mom or Cody.'

Richie knew when there was a long pause between texts that Andy was coming up with a plan, and he did. He told Richie that he had heard from his pap that people exposed got sick in a day. Andy assured Richie he probably wasn't sick or exposed, but if he wanted to be careful, he had to leave the car and walk back a couple miles.

Bailey's RV. It was parked on the edge of Bailey's property, far enough away from Hartworth to be safe. It was the place that Del had planned to meet Tanya and her son, Tad.

Andy told him to go there and he would drop off supplies and food. He also instructed Richie to turn off his phone once he let Andy know he arrived at the RV to conserve battery power. If after two days Richie showed no signs of the illness, Andy would come and get him.

But what if he did? What if he got sick?

Andy assured him that he would come.

Richie shut down his phone as he walked the distance to Bailey's property. Four miles was a long haul, especially in the dead of winter. The temperatures had dropped, and snow fell. His fingers grew numb, and his feet were wet. By the time he arrived at Bailey's property, Richie could barely feel any of his body. He was numb, but the cold didn't numb his fear. Richie was scared.

The RV looked barren; no footprints were around it at all. It was a nice RV, big and modern. Richie reached for the side screen door. It was open, but as he reached for the handle, he realized that it was locked.

He stepped back, figuring he'd try a window when the door creaked open and the barrel of a shotgun appeared.

Did someone speak? As usual, he heard something, a muffled noise similar to a tone. All Richie could do was cover his ears and call out, "I'm deaf. I'm not sick. Please. I'm cold."

After a few moments, the door opened slowly, and Richie stepped inside. An older man immediately shut the door behind Richie. He visually examined Richie then lowered the gun. He waved his hand for him to come in further.

The older man wasn't alone. The RV had at least eight people huddled together. None of them looked sick, but then again, what did Richie know.

He walked into either a safe haven or a viral time bomb.

◇◇◇◇

Lincoln, Montana

"No, Andy, listen. These are just Hazmat coveralls; they won't work keeping out a virus. They won't,"

Emma told him. "These are designed for dust. I got these for when Yellowstone blew, for the dust and debris."

In her kitchen, Andy handed her a roll of duck tape. "Seal me over the … g-gloves."

Nose running from crying, Emma did as instructed. She packed a box of supplies for Andy to take along with a five gallon container of disinfectant.

After she sealed his boots and gloves, Andy stepped into a second suit. "It … it will work."

"Keep your eyes covered with the goggles. Use the mini tank for breathing," she instructed. "Park the truck a good distance, take only the disinfectant and supplies. Got that?"

He grabbed her hand. "I'll b … be fine. I don't th … think Richie will get s … sick. Bailey's is f… four miles out."

"Be careful, and please, do not go into Hartworth."

Andy shook his head as his answer, leaned forward and kissed Emma, and then he kissed Cody. He grabbed the box of supplies and headed out. Everything else was in his truck.

After he left, Emma settled at the kitchen table with Cody. The little girl ate her lunch, oblivious to everything going on.

"You're so lucky," Emma told her. "Gam loves you so much, and I am so sorry that you are going through this."

"Gam sad?"

"Gam very sad." Emma reached out and ran her fingers down Cody's cheek. She was grateful that the child wasn't sick and that she was so young that she wouldn't remember anything. That was, if they survived whatever it was that was wiping out a town so close by.

◇◇◇◇

Hartworth, Montana

The roads were desolate; Andy expected as much. Traffic on the road was mainly between Lincoln and Hartworth, and he imagined that most in Lincoln were aware of the shut down and stayed away.

He moved pretty well despite the fact that the roads were getting slick with snow. He parked off the road where he knew he could get out, left the truck, trotted a bit, set down the sealed bag of clothes and disinfectant, and then with the supplies made his way to Bailey's RV. It was cold; the double suits did little to shield the temperature. He dreaded the thought of undressing, but it had to be done.

He set the items by the door, knocked, and took off.

Once he arrived back at the disinfectant, he undressed completely and doused his naked body with the cleaner. He shivered out of control, was barely able to breathe, and knew he faced hypothermia. Grabbing the clothes from the bag was a struggle; it was even harder putting them on since his damp body started to freeze. Once he dressed, he took off for the truck. He wore only socks, socks he took off once he returned to his vehicle, and pulled on shoes.

Andy was freezing; he didn't think he'd ever warm up. He was glad to see the message from Richie, stating, 'Thank you. Phone going off. If you don't hear from me, I did not get sick. Text on the 20th.'

Andy was confident Richie wouldn't get sick. How could he? He really wasn't exposed. Not that Andy knew.

He blasted the heat in the truck as high and hard as he could and made the fatal mistake of driving through Lincoln on the way back.

He just wanted to get back.

The second he drove into town, Andy reached for the heat, shut it off, and closed the vents.

It was surreal. Early afternoon and not a soul walked the streets. There wasn't a track in the road, not a footprint. Bonnie's was closed and so was every other business.

No movement. It was eerily empty.

Either Lincoln was scared and they hunkered down or they, too, were hit with whatever Hartworth had.

Andy didn't want to think about the latter; he just hoped for the best and drove to Emma's.

Chapter Eleven

Hartworth, Montana

December 19th

Never could he recall ever being too sick to move, yet Stew didn't move from that chair next to Heather's bed. By late afternoon, he was too sick to think. His stomach wrenched, and Stew swore he could feel the blood move through his veins. It was thick and sluggish, and it burned. His skin was so itchy he wanted to rip it from his body.

He was unable to contact Emma any longer. His phone died. However, he had a plan. To initiate it, he needed to rest. He hoped that would give him one more boost of strength. But Stew closed his eyes to sleep and didn't wake up until it was dark. The clock read after midnight. How much time had passed, had been wasted. He wondered if he should even attempt his plan. As he reached his hand toward Heather, he heard confirmation that he should.

Sobs.

Stew didn't need to see who was crying; he knew. It was Val, and he also knew the reason; Roman had to have passed away. Stew looked down to Heather. She was barely responsive, and Stew realized that she wasn't far behind.

With every ounce of strength he had, he slipped his hands under Heather and lifted her as he stood to his feet. Stew teetered. The weight of her body on his arms was like hot coals, burning, aching, and straight through to every nerve fiber in his body.

Walking would be a chore, and he did so one step at a time. He swayed a lot, bumped into the wall, but Stew kept moving.

His legs hurt like hell as he stumbled toward the stairs. He prayed with every step he took that he wouldn't drop his granddaughter.

"Stew," Val called out weakly. "Where are you going?"

Stew glanced only a second over his shoulder and moved for the staircase. "We're both dying," Stew said. "We're going home."

The steps were the biggest obstacle. Using the walls as support, Stew glided down more than walked. He even stumbled twice. He imagined it was the last of his determination that kept him going. He just needed to get outside. Val would certainly have a car there, something, and then Stew could go back in for the keys after he got Heather in the car.

He didn't expect for Larry to pull up in the squad car.

"Where ya headed, Stew? You look bad."

"I feel bad, Larry. I'm heading home. I'm taking my baby and we're heading home to die."

"You can't leave Hartworth."

"The hell I can't. I can go home. My property is far enough away from Lincoln. I'll go straight there. I'll open the propane and once my girl passes, it's done. But I'm not gonna die here, and neither is she. Not here." Larry looked forward and then Larry stepped from the police car, leaving the door open. He walked to Stew. "Give me the girl."

Stew shook his head.

"Give her to me, Stew. I'll put her in my car. Keys are in the ignition. Just give me your word you go only to your house and you do just as you told me."

"You have my word."

"Then you take my car." Larry braced under Heather and lifted her from Stew.

The release of the weight was a relief, and Stew walked slowly to the driver's side. As he slid in, Larry set Heather in the passenger's seat, buckled the belt, and closed the door. Stew could barely grip the door enough to close it. Larry walked over.

"Godspeed, Stew. Find peace."

Stew nodded. Then Larry closed the door. The car was running, and Stew drove off.

Larry stood there watching until the police car drove from his sight. When he turned, Val stood there.

Val didn't wear a coat. His face was drawn, and he handed Larry the journal.

"Why are you giving me this?"

"To take it back to the fire hall. But I see you have to walk now."

Larry shrugged. "No big deal." He inhaled as he took the journal. "My, uh, my work is done. You ok?"

"No. No, not at all. But …my work is done, too." After a heavy sigh, Val turned and walked back into his house.

Holding that journal, Larry began his walk back to the fire hall. He was barely a block down the empty, quiet street when the sound of a single shot ring out. Larry stopped. He knew what it was and from what direction it came, but he paused briefly to look over his shoulder, and then Larry kept walking.

FLASH FORWARD

Ground Zero – 9

December 23rd

Hartworth, Montana

In the time it took for Edward to cross the street to the expedient lab, the forces had arrived. Massive numbers of vehicles pulled into town, and Edward instructed them to get situated and wait for his directives on the search. He knew the teams would search and retrieve as they combed through every square inch of Hartworth and beyond.

But first, the town doctor.

He had to be the one, Edward figured, who wrote the journal. It was too precise about too many things. Edward grabbed the journal on the way to the town doctor's place.

The doctor's office was located on the bottom floor of the house; Edward's initial team was there, all four of them. He went upstairs and entered the bedroom where Goldman waited. There were two single beds; the body of a younger man, decimated by the illness, was on one bed, and next to him was the body of an older man. He had a single gunshot wound to his head.

"Makes no sense," Goldman said. "The other bed shows signs that someone else was sick. There are syringes. Towels. The other bedroom as well. Yet, only the boy has the virus."

Edward stepped closer. "Do we have a name?"

"Vladimir Paltrov. Russian immigrant, came to the US thirty plus years ago. He was an easy run, ran his name while waiting on you. He was under constant observation for about ten years. A doctor in Russia was always in contact there."

Martha entered the room and handed the journal to Edward. "Handwriting is a match on the charts downstairs."

Edward crouched down for a closer examination. "He has to be the one that brought it in. Has to be. But I thought Ebolapox wasn't invented until the 1990s."

"No," Goldman said. "Some say 1976. Remember we have nothing. It was a paper study."

"This is our man. Not a sign of the virus," Edward said. "The other patient may have been moved to the fire hall. Who knows? But this other guy … do we know his name?" He indicated the young man.

"Roman Paltrov. Son."

"Also patient zero," Edward said. "Look at the nose; it deteriorated from the disease. We hadn't seen a single victim like him. He's the furthest along. Bet he was first. So he's patient zero. This explains all the medical attention in this room." Edward stood. "It's sort of piecing together. Paltrov had the bug here somewhere. The son found it. Released it. Paltrov knew it, and that explains why they shut the town down."

Martha interjected, "That doesn't explain why the sheriff nor the doctor showed no symptoms."

"He's easy," Edward said. "He had an inoculation. Surely, there isn't an antidote or the son wouldn't be sick. No, there's a vaccine for this. Bet me. I can't be sure about the sheriff. But him … this helps. If this is his, and this was, as we think, a Cold War bio-weapon, then maybe the Soviets have an answer to this bug if it gets out of control or if it broke barriers."

"Hey, Ed," Harold called out. "We got a problem." He turned holding a wallet. "This belongs to the son. What day did you determine was the release date?"

Edward answered, "December 16th." He looked at Harold and extended his hand. "What is that?"

"Concert ticket stubs," Harold answered. "At eight p.m., he and someone else went to a concert in Billings."

"Don't tell me."

Harold gave him the stubs. "December 16th."

Edward glanced at the ticket stubs, to the bed, and then back to the date of the concert. "Let's just hope I'm wrong on the date. If I'm not, let's hope this release happened after this concert."

Chapter Twelve

Lincoln, Montana

December 19th

There were three sounds in Emma's living room: the crackling fire, the sniffles of sadness, and the nearly silent shuffling of papers.

Emma sat on a small footstool with a box before her, and next to that a stack of photographs. She looked at each one, and then placed it in the box.

The hour was late, but she wasn't tired. Cody slept on the couch. Emma ceased letting the child out of her sight. Andy just sat and listened.

She hadn't heard from her father all day. Last conversation, Stew called Andy. That was it. Emma had given up hope.

"This is my life," Emma told Andy. "I'm going to spend the rest of the night just writing the story of my life," she spoke sadly. "That way, if someone finds it, whether they're officials, people in the future, or another civilization, they'll know. They'll look at this and see people lived and were loved in this world. We just didn't make it."

Andy reached out and grabbed her wrists. "It's n … not over."

"Not yet," Emma said. "This is the big one, Andy. People always think I'm crazy with this end of the world shit, but this is the big one. It took a town, now Lincoln is under. You said you called Bob in Mead; they have it there." She shook her head. "Heather called me in the morning sick. She went to Billings the night before. Now ... either she caught it in Billings, or she was sick when she went. In either case, it's in Billings. Yeah … we may be fine for now. We may even be able to outrun it. Stay ahead of it. But eventually, it will catch us when we have nowhere else to run."

"May … may be-be a cure?"

"Maybe," Emma said. "But it could be too late. Bet me in a week the West Coast is down. If it is in Billings, it's made it out of Billings. Someone took it elsewhere." She winced as if in pain. "Planes. One plane ride. But …" she sighed. "It doesn't matter. I always thought it would. I always thought I'd care, that I'd want to survive. But honestly … my daughter is dying, if not already gone."

"Cody … n-needs you."

"What kind of life would it be?"

"What … ev … ever you m … make it for her. R-Richie is not s-sick."

Emma nodded. Her eyes lifted when a light from outside flashed. She stood and turned to the window. "Headlights?"

Andy stood and joined Emma at the window. The vehicle began to back from the driveway, flicking its lights. Andy and Emma rushed to the front door. As soon as they opened it, a squeal of feedback rang out in the dead silent dark.

Then they heard Stew's weak voice. "We're heading to the main house," he said over the speaker. "I'll park out front. Dress warm and wear gloves and masks. We'll be in the car. You can't touch us. You can get near the car." Pause. "It's time to say goodbye."

The car backed up and pulled away.

They rushed. They moved as fast as they could to pull on coats and hats, and scarves to cover their mouths. Emma understood she couldn't hold her daughter or even touch her, kiss her, but she could see her. She could see her daughter and father. It was a gift. A sad one, but still a gift.

They took Andy's truck up the road to Stew's house. The police car parked sideways out front with the lights blinking.

Cody was half-asleep in Emma's arms; she opened the door and stepped out with Andy. She could see the two figures in the car as she walked closer. She lost every bit of her breath and clutched Cody tighter when she saw her father and Heather. Her dad looked bad, really bad, but Heather … It crushed Emma to see her, and she felt her heart squeeze in pain as she ached out a cry that echoed in the night, a cry of pain that only a mother could make.

Her daughter. Her poor, sweet little girl, a child that Emma tried to protect yet at that moment was unable to help at all.

"Hey," Stew spoke through the speaker. "We don't have much time. Heather … she doesn't have much time. I'm glad we made it. We had to see you. I ...I had to see you, Em."

Another whimper slipped from Emma as she walked closer to the car. Heather leaned against the window, her eyes closed. Then Heather opened her eyes. When she did, it was as if the girl had renewed strength. Her hand lifted to the window and Heather burst into tears as her fingers scraped the glass as if to feel Cody.

"My baby." Heather's muffled words carried from the car. "Cody, Mommy loves you. I love you. Mom, I'm sorry."

"No. No." Emma shook her head. "Why are you sorry?"

"For putting you through this." Heather's shoulders bounced as she cried then her head went back as she breathed heavily.

Stew extended the microphone to Heather.

Squeal.

"Mommy, protect my baby. Please. Protect my baby. I love you."

Emma handed the baby to Andy and raced to the car; she dropped to her knees and put her hand on the window. "Heather. Honey, I love you, baby. I wish I could touch you. Hold you. Take it away."

"It's okay." Heather turned her body and put her hand back on the window. She held it there.

Emma raised her hand to meet Heather's against that window.

"Emma," Stew said, his words breathy and weak. "I am so proud of you. Please know that. I have always been .... Always been proud of you. I … I love you." He dropped the microphone and after a squeal, Stew turned into toward Heather placing his hand on the glass as well, next to Heather's.

Emma positioned her hand between theirs, wishing with all her might she could touch them, hold them. It was without a doubt her goodbye to her father and her child.

Then Heather's hand slid down the window, and her head dropped to the side.

"No." Emma pounded on the window. "Heather. Heather." She smacked the glass. "No!" She sobbed loudly as she watched her father grab and hold Heather, his strong body bouncing in his own anguish.

With his free hand, Stew grabbed the microphone. "Go home, Emma. Be safe. Now. Andy, take them. I need to get in the house."

Emma cried out repeatedly as Andy grabbed hold of her.

"Cody … d … doesn't need this." Andy told her. "Come. I'm s… so … sorry."

Emma, despite her efforts to stay, was pulled back. She finally gave in and got into Andy's truck.

"Gam? Mommy?" Cody asked groggily. "Mommy?"

"Mommy's with Pap." Emma kissed Cody. Her tears fell, saturating her face. Her soul was weak; she could barely breathe, her emotions were so thick.

Andy got into the truck as well.

He put the truck in gear and started to back up.

"Wait." Emma grabbed his arm. "Let me watch them go in the house. Please?"

Andy stopped the truck and nodded.

Emma watched as Stew stepped from the car. She seeped a cry at the way he walked and moved. Stew opened the passenger's door, reached in, and awkwardly lifted Heather with an apparent struggle. Emma realized her error in asking to stay, when Stew toppled to the ground and Andy whipped open the door.

"Andy?" Emma called his name.

Andy shut the door, paused, leaned forward, kissed Cody, and then placed his hand on Emma's cheek. "I love you." He placed his lips softly to hers. "Be strong."

Before Emma could comprehend why he was saying it, the truck door opened, Andy stepped out, and closed the door.

He took two steps, faced Emma, lifted his hand in a wave, then turned around and rushed to Stew.

It was at that very second, watching Andy help her father that Emma knew that she didn't just say goodbye to her father and child, she had just said goodbye to Andy, as well.

FINAL FLASH FORWARD

Ground Zero – 10

December 23rd

Hartworth, Montana

For the first time in hours, Edward decontaminated and sat in his special office in the lab, an environmentally controlled area that he felt was safe from any 'Hartworth' air. His eyes shifted to the activity outside the lab. He monitored it through the computer screen while speaking to Bill Lange on the speakerphone.

He knew he'd have to get suited up again. However, first he needed coffee. The eight hours there seemed like days.

"Secretary of State has already been in contact with the Soviet Prime Minister," Lange said. "They're working with the Soviet weapons commission to see if this is theirs."

Edward scoffed a tired laugh. "Of course it's theirs. Christ. Dr. Paltrov, whatever his real name is, came from there. He worked there, constantly communicated with them."

"I know. But it isn't our job to accuse the Soviet Union of withholding information or covering it up."

"They must just not know, or they think it was destroyed," Edward suggested. "Who in the hell would allow humanity to get devastated by a virus if they could stop it?"

"Maybe they can't," Lange suggested. "Maybe the only one who could shot himself in the head."

Edward grumbled.

"Ed, we have to start working on this stat, you know it. If there was a higher level than level four, this would be it. This is a lock down project."

"I know."

"Probability is high, Ed, that these cases in Billings are EPV-571."

"I know they are, especially after seeing those concert tickets," Edward said. "I knew we'd get reports after that bulletin, but I didn't expect it so fast."

"The reports were in before the bulletin, they just were in queue with every other health incident that gets reported. They weren't flagged until we looked."

Edward sighed. "I'm wrapped up in this town. How many now?"

"Ninety-one cases, thirty deaths in Billings. Numbers gonna grow. That's not including the five in Seattle."

"So all the trouble this guy went through to seal this town was in vain. We could have been brought in days ago."

"Yep," Lange replied. "But could we stop it?"

"I don't know if anything can stop this. I don't even want to think about three days from now."

"I already have Walker on this. Hopefully he'll crack it soon."

Edward nodded, not as if Lange could see him. He then noticed someone waving to the camera. He turned up the volume.

"Dr. Neil!" The worker called through his suit. "You have to see this. We are locking it on now."

"Be right out." Edward said then turned his attention back to the phone. "Bill, I have to call you back. They found something."

He ended the call and looked at the computer one more time. He watched crew workers carrying a long tube, a large flexible tube, not easily maneuvered. It was a safe way, a walkway from one safe area to the next.

Edward suited up and left the lab. The safe way was already sealed to a CDC mobile truck, sealed to the airtight compartment. The other end of the tubing was closed tight until it was locked in or latched to its destination.

The truck was parked outside of the police station.

When Edward arrived, the crews already had the tubing inside and down the basement door. He couldn't get through.

"What's going on?" Edward asked.

"We were combing," a worker said. "We went downstairs to the holding area and noticed a door was shut to the holding cells. When we looked through, we saw a survivor. Not sick. We didn't want to chance opening that door in case it kept out the germ. We're almost hooked up. We have someone suited up down there."

"Walk them through to the truck?" Edward asked.

"Yes, sir. Getting the bubble ready. He'll walk right into that."

"Good. Good," Edward said with a swat to the worker's back. "He or she survived this long, let's keep them safe as possible. Better yet, maybe they're immune."

The prospect of a survivor in the dead town renewed Edward's hope. If the individual was immune, then others would be, too, and the odds of defeating EBV-571 grew.

He headed from the police station to the truck and waited inside.

The survivor would walk straight up the ramp, through the tube, into a plastic cage, a protective bubble with its own air supply.

Edward anxiously awaited the survivor.

◇◇◇◇

'Patient seems to be in fair condition,' Edward noted in his computer, notes he would send directly to the CDC. *'He is slightly lethargic and fades in and out of a conscious state. He exhibits signs of confusion.*

This is attributed to hypothermia and dehydration. He shows no outward sign of the virus but does have an insignificant flesh wound on the lumbar region. Patient claims it is a gunshot wound and a safety/survival belt prohibited the penetration of the bullet. It is noted that Doctor Monroe did find a large belt in the holding cell. It is difficult to fully assess patient because of protective surroundings. Patient claims he tended to the wound and has been in the holding area of the police station for six days. He has eaten, but states it became difficult to swallow once his water supply had finished. Observation and testing is recommended.'

Edward finished his notes, hit send, and stood. He turned to the protective bubble. The man inside sat against the wall, his knees brought close. "Mr. Lewiskowski."

He lifted his head. "Del. Just … call me Del."

"Del. This is where I'll leave you for now. I apologize for the protective room, but it's needed. We don't know if you were exposed to or were shielded from the virus. However, we are transporting you now. Give us a few hours and I promise to make you more comfortable."

"Where am I going?"

"Atlanta, to our facility there. It is best."

Del's head lifted. "Atlanta? I'm not sick. Just … just been in that cell too long."

"Yes, well, you happened to also be the only person left alive in Hartworth."

Immediately, Del's head dropped to his knees and his arms wrapped around his legs. He released a quiet sob.

"Are you all right?" Edward asked.

"My daughter was here in this town."

Edward felt his breath leave him. As a father, he could relate to what Del felt. "I am very sorry. So you're from here?"

Del shook his head. "No. I was on my way to find her. That's when they got me. At the roadblock. I'm from Lincoln."

"I see."

"Is Lincoln okay?" Del asked.

Edward lifted his hands. "I honestly cannot tell you because I don't know. I will soon, though. That's where I'm headed."

"Is there any way you can get word to me?" Del asked. "My son is there. My granddaughter."

"I'll get word." Edward watched Del rest back and close his eyes in exhaustion and sadness. He excused himself, wished Del luck, and left the trailer. He'd more than likely see Del again when he returned to Atlanta. However, first Edward had a stop to make.

Lincoln, Montana was next on his list.

◇◇◇◇

The home in Hartworth that placed that final call was empty. That's what Edward was told as he and

Harold made their way to Lincoln. It was forty miles north; they were hopeful, but not for long.

Edward knew as soon as they passed the 'Lincoln Five Miles' sign. The roads were snow-covered and untouched. Not a single tire track. As they rolled into town that late afternoon, it was a repeat of the nightmare in Hartworth.

Only there was no roadblock with a dead man holding a gun. There was nothing. No lights. No automatic Christmas music chiming in the silence. In fact, the town had no indication of Christmas at all. Nothing. It was snow-covered, dark, and dismal.

It was a two-block, one-stoplight town, and they barely made it down the first block when Harold hit the brakes.

Edward was too busy looking around to notice. However, Harold did.

At the end of the second block, a man stood by a large truck.

"What the hell?" Edward asked then opened the car door. He checked his suit connections and stepped out.

Harold joined him.

The man walked further away from the truck and more into view in the center of the street, and as Edward and Harold neared him, he dropped to his knees and his head hung forward. It looked as if he collapsed in emotional exhaustion more than anything else, but Edward couldn't be sure.

He and Harold raced his way. When he arrived, he expected the man to lift his head and show how sick he was. But when Edward called out, 'I'm Dr. Edward Neil from the Centers for Disease Control. Are you okay?' the man shook his head and looked up.

Edward gasped.

He wasn't sick. Not at all.

"Are you ill?" Harold asked.

He shook his head again and brought his hand to his face. The man then began to cry. Was it out of relief, sadness, and exhaustion, or all of the above?

Edward asked. "What happened here? Where is everyone?"

The man, without looking, only pointed to the truck.

Edward walked to the large construction dump truck. As he approached, he saw another truck around the corner. He could only assume that truck was the same as the one before him.

The entire back portion as filled with bodies. Edward only needed to look at one victim, just one, to know what killed them.

"It's ours," Harold said.

Edward returned to the man. "Everyone?"

He nodded.

"Everyone in town?"

Another nod.

"You handled these bodies, you were around during this all, and you aren't sick?"

"No," he finally spoke.

"Were you ever?"

He shook his head.

After a deep breath, Edward extended his hand to the man. “I need you to come with us. Okay? You’ll have to come with us.”

Slowly the man stood.

“What is your name?”

“An … Andy.”

“Andrew Jenkins?”

Andy gave a surprised look to Edward.

Repeating, “Come with us,” Edward led him toward their SUV.

Andy Jenkins was not sick. Unlike Del, he was out in the open and dealt with the ill and bodies yet did not succumb at all. Why?

Edward immediately put faith in Andy Jenkins, the lone survivor of Lincoln, Montana. Faith that Andy held answers Edward needed. He wasn’t ill; somewhere in his body could be a clue to defeating the deadliest thing Edward ever witnessed. Not only that, but Andy was also the last person to talk to anyone in Hartworth.

Andy Jenkins received that last call.

Chapter Thirteen

Atlanta, GA

December 23rd

"See ya next year," Dr. Chad Walker cheerfully told his wife as he placed the remaining items into his duffel bag and case.

His wife of eighteen years grumbled, lifted her bourbon glass, and said, "Whatever."

"I'll call when I can," Chad said, grabbing his things.

"If I don't answer, I may be having multiple affairs."

"I'm sure you will. Enjoy." Smugly, Chad walked out. Where others would hate the thought of where he was going, Chad looked forward to it. Any time away from Belinda was a vacation.

A car was waiting for him outside. Chad was tall and lanky with a small drinker's gut. He gave the driver his bags and got inside. While he wasn't pompous, he spoke as if he was. Educated and brilliant, he had almost an aristocratic dialect.

The driver got in the car. "Shouldn't take long to get there. Rush hour traffic is light today for some odd reason."

"It may get lighter."

"I'm sorry?"

Chad shook his head. "Bad humor. Can we swing by a liquor store, please?"

"Sure thing."

Not that there wouldn't be an ample supply of adult beverages, but Chad wanted to make sure he had his own. It was going to be a long stay.

If anyone could be labeled beyond super intelligent, it was Chad. The CDC knew it, which was why they paid him the big bucks and, more so, why they called him in.

Chad was always years beyond the others when growing up, but his parents refused to move him ahead, so Chad trumped the others in intelligence then made money off of it by selling answers to homework and doing essays.

When he was fourteen, his school bus passed a dog hit by a car. The female dog was pregnant, and Chad, pulled out his pocketknife and did an emergency caesarian on the dog right there on the side of the road, while his classmates watched. He saved two of the puppies, but unfortunately, authorities didn't see his heroics; he spent six months in a juvenile delinquent center for animal mutilation. It didn't hurt him; Chad was so likable he defeated the odds inside the center.

He wasn't a target, so he wasn't beat up. When threatened he outsmarted and learned how to deal with all kinds of people.

Those skills helped him, and they would help him in his next endeavor.

It wasn't the first time Chad was going into what he like to call the 'Doomsday' lab, a biological protection facility that ran on an old fashion color-coded level system. Aside from security and maintenance and food workers, the staff was four men, four women. A couple doctors, nurses, scientists such as Chad, and, of course, the subjects who donated their blood and time for the cause.

In the event of a biological incident or pandemic threat, those in the facility would live there under lock down, work on the virus, attempt to find a possible cure or solution until the threat was over and the level dropped to yellow, or the designated 'burnout' time frame of 160 days has passed, then the facility would be unlocked. Until then, there was no way out.

Only a couple of times in his career had it gotten to a level red, but the longest Chad was sealed in was thirty-three days. He didn't suspect it would be the case with the current bug.

It went from green to yellow to orange in eight hours.

Eight hours. From the arrival time at Hartworth to the lift off of the survivors, eight hours had passed. In a matter of days, four states had been affected, and Chad expected more.

His job wasn't only to beat it, stop it, but find out how it got that far that fast. If it moved in a few days to that many areas, it was only a matter of weeks before it went global.

To say it hadn't left the West Coast, although nothing was confirmed on the East Coast or anywhere else for that matter, was insane. It hadn't been that long; Chad was certain it was out.

Level red or code red wasn't days away, but hours.

He just hoped that Edward Neil was moved to the facility before it automatically shut down.

Ed was fun to work with.

There were a few things arriving from Montana: two survivors, the journal, and 'live' samples. Chad wanted to be at 'Doomsday' before they arrived, be there and set up, but he only had a short period of time before that happened.

During the car ride to the liquor store and then the facility, Chad reviewed his notes and pictures again about the virus on his computer pad.

Ebolapox, as they called, it was baffling and sickening. Someone created it, yet he didn't think anyone would step forward. He hoped they would.

In any of the times in lock down, never was it a question of what it meant if time ran out.

The burnout time didn't just mean the threat of the virus burned out, it meant humanity did, too. Enough people lost their lives that there weren't enough hosts left to carry it. In that situation, society surely was done. Life outside the facility would have changed, and not for the better.

Chad never really gave much thought to that scenario, because he never really saw that as an option. A cure would be found, or the virus would lose power.

However, the current one worried Chad. Ebolapox very well could be unbeatable. It moved too fast and spread too widely for it to be trapped, caught, and cured before too much damage was done. It was like being in a Dodge in a race against a Ferrari. That's how Chad felt, and it was the first time ever that he honestly saw the burnout as a real possibility.

◇◇◇◇

Hartworth, Montana

Edward was just about to rub his eyes, but he stopped. He resisted because he didn't want to take a chance that even something miniscule would make it through the mucus membrane of the eyes.

It was pushing evening, and they sat in a makeshift meeting room two miles outside of Hartworth in a CDC mobile.

"Where are we?" Edward asked.

Goldman spoke first. "Bodies are being gathered. Be done tomorrow. Town is scheduled for demolition day after Christmas. Preliminary autopsy and testing are done on the doctor and sheriff. Both had the same immunities to the virus. Interestingly enough, not only did both of them have the standard smallpox vaccine scar, they both had an inoculation site which looked similar to the smallpox scar, only dark."

Edward lifted his head. "So it's pretty much confirmed there was an inoculation. But why the sheriff? Were they able to determine how long ago he was inoculated?"

Goldman shook his head. "Not exactly, but it wasn't recent. It was before the release."

"Martha," Edward said. "Numbers."

"Not good. Billings alone has over two hundred confirmed cases; death toll has also increased. Reported cases in Washington, Iowa, North Dakota, California, and Nevada. Interestingly enough, we haven't found a single person that went to that concert."

"That's because the ones exposed at the concert are dead," Edward said. "Air samples."

"You'll like this," Martha replied with a hint of sarcasm. "Small concentration of the virus in 80% of bio air samples taken in town. In Lincoln, the virus shows up in five out of every ten. Billings, even outside of the concert area, we are getting four out of ten. The good news is that in Lincoln the virus in the samples is dead. So it died out shortly after the people."

"Billings?"

"Alive," Martha replied. "Because people are still sick there. It is not a safe area."

"Christ." Edward exhaled. "Hartworth."

"Alive."

"How can that be?" Edward asked. "Everyone is dead."

"Because it's still leaking from somewhere. It is the highest concentration out of all locations. In addition, the doctor's house is a hot zone. Alive and thriving."

"So it's there," Edward pointed. "We have to find it before we bulldoze this town. We don't need the weapon buried for a future generation to find and open this Pandora's Box all over again."

"We're on it."

Edward looked over to Harold. "You're being quiet. What's up?"

"Studying our patient zero. I think I theoretically know how this thing got out of control."

Edward gave a sarcastic scoff. "The concert."

"Most part," Harold stated. "But let's say they were in contact with a few hundred. That would spread it, but not as rapidly to other states like it has been going. Roman was here at the clinic. The last note he made was around 2:30. A patient came in; he marked them off. His debit card was used at a fast food restaurant ten miles from here."

Edward closed his eyes and groaned. "They stopped for take out."

"And then he checked into the Brightside Motel. His debit card was swiped at 5:00 p.m. Brightside is a fleabag motel off the highway. Mainly truckers, which could account for odd locations of the virus popping up. But I tried to contact the motel and … it burned down."

Edward's attention as caught. "It burned down. When?"

"December 16th. Arson. Someone deliberately set it on fire. Killed everyone. Interestingly enough, Roman is in the computer records and is listed as deceased because his car was still in the lot."

Martha spoke up. "So he and his friend were probably sick, and whoever picked them up, lit the place. Had to be the dad or the sheriff. They locked down Hartworth. They knew Roman had the virus and tried to stop it there."

"Exactly," Harold said. "It's my theory that since this thing is a weapon and it is distributed by missiles, it isn't heat resistant."

"Wouldn't the doctor know this?" Edward asked.

Harold nodded. "Yes. But I'm betting he thought only the actual weapon was resistant to heat. Come on, the germ levels in this town tell how strong this thing is."

Edward sighed. "So instead of destroying it, he created a pseudo bomb with the fire."

Harold again nodded. "And the smoke carried it. Yep."

"Oh my God." Edward spun and picked up the phone. "This thing is now in the red level." He dialed. "And unfortunately it's been there longer than we even knew."

◇◇◇◇

Atlanta, GA

Andy was in a whirlwind emotionally and physically. One minute he was walking through the desolate town of Lincoln filled with despair, the next he was whisked off. Stuffed in a plastic bag, stripped of his clothing, scrubbed and scrubbed again then put into a room.

The room wasn't that bad. It had a bed, dresser, small couch, and table. There was a private bathroom, a computer, and a television with cable. It would have been perfect had it not been for the fact that Andy couldn't get out.

He had been there for hours. They brought him food, clothes, took his blood. They talked to him only briefly. He was clueless as to what was going on. They said very little.

Andy wasn't in a good state of mind, not at all. He was still drowning in pain over all that happened.

He didn't regret the decision to help Stew because he knew Stew would have done the same for him. When Stew fell, Andy rushed to help him stand, and then he carried Heather's body inside and returned for Stew.

Stew was ravaged with the illness, and Andy couldn't leave his side. He wiped him down, gave him water, and then watched him die. Stew vomited so much there was nothing left but blood. His body was black and had expanded so much that his skin peeled and ripped. The final moments of his life were a few short labored breaths, a stare, and Stew was gone.

He died early in the morning on the 20th. The ground was too cold to bury them, and Andy didn't want to take a chance of throwing the virus into the air by burning them. So he planned to return. He turned off the heat. The winter would serve as a freezer.

Andy stayed in the house until the next morning, but he knew. He could see Emma's house from Stew's and there hadn't been a light on in over a day.

He didn't want to take a chance that the germ was on him, and Andy had no plans to touch Emma, but he wanted to talk to her.

He walked to the house, knocked, peeked in the window, and then went inside.

He was too late.

Emma and Cody were gone.

Andy felt bad that he wasn't there for them. Wasn't there to help them. In fact, Andy was too late for anyone in Lincoln.

His truck was still parked outside of Emma's, and he took that into town.

Barren. Dark. He went house to house, but everyone was either dead or close to it.

He was stuck in those memories, the feeling of great sadness, when the sound of a buzz caught his attention.

It was the door. Andy heard that sound before. Only this time, a man walked in without a protective suit.

The man carried a bottle of whiskey.

"Mr. Jenkins, congratulations. Not only are you not a carrier, but you are completely immune to this thing. We don't know why or how, we'll find out, but for now, I thought maybe you'd like a nightcap."

Andy nodded.

"Good." He walked to the table. "My name is Dr. Chad Walker. I am the facilitator and head virologist here." He grabbed a glass and paused to look at the plate of food. "You haven't eaten."

"N … not hung … hung … grrr . Hungry."

"I see." Chad poured a small amount of whiskey for Andy and handed him the glass. "I have to say I am a huge fan of your work. The Ice Age Baby. Brilliant."

"Th … thank you."

"I'm a writer as well. I wrote about germ warfare. I thought it was brilliant. However … my best royalty year was three hundred dollars. You?"

"Twelve hun … hundred."

"Well, you and I both know we write for the love of it. You can't make a living being an author, unless you're Stephen King. And … I'll leave the bottle here for you. There's a nice documentary on the History channel tonight about Bog People. You may enjoy it."

Andy nodded.

"I realize this is an inconvenience," Chad said. "You feel trapped. I know. I promise it won't be for long. Some testing, some interviews, and before long you'll be free to move about the facility. Can I just get your patience and cooperation for a few days?"

"Yes."

"Good." Chad snapped his fingers and reached into his pocket. He set down a pill bottle. "For you. Once a day. Take it with breakfast and eat."

"I'm n … not s-s-sick."

"That's not for illness. It's for the stutter. With all the emotional trauma you have been through the last thing you need is to feel frustrated during the interviews. It won't get rid of the stutter completely, but it will take a lot of the edge off. It works on that portion of the brain. I'm surprised no one has given you medication."

"Th .. they d-did. I … c … couldn't afford it," Andy said.

"Ah, there we go again. The negatives of the literary life." Chad walked to the door. "I know you have been through a harrowing experience. You'll have to relive it via interviews with us and for that I apologize. That's why we aren't asking too many questions tonight. You rest. Please. Enjoy the whiskey."

"How … how … long?" Andy asked.

Chad paused before leaving. "How long will you be here?" He shrugged. "I don't know. This bug is lethal, as you know, and this stay could be longer than both of us would like. Have a good night."

The doctor left, and Andy took a sip of his drink.

He'd make the best of it; try to not think about Lincoln too much, especially since he had to talk about it a lot. Perhaps he'd even get a little tipsy; that would help him sleep. Andy needed to sleep. He hadn't done that for days.

Chapter Fourteen
Atlanta, GA

December 24th

Del drew the curtain over the glass wall for privacy. He recognized the man they brought into the next isolation room. He was the doctor that interviewed him on the CDC truck. Del waved to him, but really, Del didn't want to be bothered by anyone.

What did he expect? That after a few days in the cell, nearly a week, he'd emerge to find the town hunky dory? He survived off the rations that Emma had given to him. He used the small first aid kit, cleaned his wound, and then used the liquid sutures to seal it. He had four doses of ibuprofen and used them sparingly.

He should have known. The increased silence, the temperature dropping, no one checking on him. No footsteps. He sat in that cell while everyone around him died.

An IV was hooked up to his arm; he had a few more days in quarantine before they let him out. Del didn't even feel like getting out of bed. Of course, the room was clinical and small, nothing more than a hospital room.

They gave him a small hand held computer. They instructed him that if he truly cared about humanity, he would use his fame to get the word out about the virus. Get people to stay in, stay safe.

The Chad guy said, "Get in touch with those one million plus likes on your social media site. Typically, we would ask you not to, but this has to be heard."

Del watched a little bit of the news. Perhaps the media was trying to be responsible, downplaying the concern. However, it was in seven states, and no one once mentioned Hartworth or Lincoln. Why?

The only word Del received about Lincoln was that there was one lone survivor and the entire town was dead.

The entire town. He even searched the web, but only conspiracy sites mentioned the dead towns.

So he wrote a blog and linked it to his social media site.

A tragedy has occurred and is still occurring all around us. Right now, this season of joy is a season of sorrow for me. I lost my entire family. They passed away from a virus that seems to be gripping this nation. If you don't know about it, look into it. I urge you. I don't want you to be me.

I am sitting here in a world of hurt drowning in a swamp of regret and pity. I chose my career over being a father. I wasn't there when they lived, and I wasn't there when they died. But just like in life, I was so close, yet did nothing. In this case, there was nothing I could do.

I missed the years of Little League and Girl Scouts. I never learned sign language to communicate with my son because a part of me believed he wasn't really deaf.

I missed the time with my daughter, my oldest child, who never gave up on me.

I never got to know the precious feeling of being a grandfather because I missed that, too.

The mother of my children was an eccentric and quirky person. She was beautiful inside and out, supported everything I did, and I left her.

Was my career so important? Looking back now, I know that it wasn't. In hindsight, being a rock star wasn't my greatest accomplishment; being a father and husband was, and I failed to see that, failed to measure up to what I could have been. I failed to be a part of what could have been more rewarding that any record deal.

I screwed up, and now I pay.

Don't be me. Embrace the ones you love. Appreciate them, tell them, and protect them.

Within minutes of posting the blog, the comments and 'likes' flooded in. Over twenty thousand likes, a thousand shares, and so many comments that Del couldn't keep up; he tried, but he grew frustrated.

Comments like …

Remember God has a reason for this. Prayers.

I know how you feel; I lost my son five years ago. I am praying for you. Jesus will pull you through.

Glad I got my flu shot.

For real? This is happening?

I am sorry for your pain.

Hugs and prayers, Del.

Is this a new song? Love it!

Really? Seriously? Del thought. All the comments and only a handful of people read beyond a few words and picked up his warning. Only a handful? They just didn't get it. They would, but at that moment, they didn't. Then again, how could Del really expect the public to 'get it' when he himself barely comprehended it at all?

◇◇◇◇

"But, Ed, it's Christmas Eve," Donna, Edward's wife, said over the phone.

"I realize this. I do. Come on, Donna. I didn't even want to chance that I harbored this thing. It's that bad. You should have left."

"Really, Ed, what is another day. They kids already don't get to see you. Uproot them on Christmas?"

"Yes, yes, uproot them and do it now. Do not wait, get someone to keep an eye on the kids, toss the toys in the car, and tell them Santa is only going to the safe house. But get there. I'm not joking; it's a six hour drive."

"This thing is scaring you."

"I have never told you to go to the safe house before. I have never been scared to be near my family. Donna, I love you guys so much. This is bad. Go."

He hoped she listened. Edward waited for another phone call to say she was on her way. The safe house was in the mountains of Virginia, nestled far away from civilization, already stocked and easily sealed.

He was frustrated and worried, but the afternoon call from Martha helped.

"We found it."

Edward relaxed into the chair. "In the doctor's office?"

"Yep. Basement. But, Ed, I have good news and bad news. What do you want first?"

"How bad is the bad news?"

"Bad," Martha said.

"Go on."

"We found the cases. Each contained enough germs to wipe out a state. Cross-checked finger prints, the son's prints were on one case, the doctor's on the rest. Ed, he .... He broke all the vials."

"Jesus."

"Fortunately, it's not carrying out of the town. However, the entire town, as you know, is a hot zone with the live virus. I was able to get a sample of the pure virus. We'll bring that with us."

"Good. What's the good news?" Edward asked.

"We immediately started testing it. We need to decontaminate this town. We don't know how long the pure germ will live in the air. Cold does nothing; it doesn't even slow it. We can't freeze the area so that's out. It's extremely heat-resistant. In fact, it reacts like a prion. Heat does nothing to it; higher temps can even multiply it."

"Can it be destroyed like a prion?" Edward asked.

"Yes," Martha replied. "We immediately took that route. Prolonged exposure of thirty minutes or more to high doses of radiation, probably 10G or more, or prolonged exposure to high temperatures."

"Don't tell me. 1,100 Fahrenheit or more."

"Yep. So one or the other is the only way to sterilize the area. Wipe out the weapon with a weapon."

"So basically, to clean Montana, we have to nuke a portion of Montana. The President will never allow this."

"He really doesn't have a choice. If he doesn't, this is a hot zone for … I don't know how long. And Ed, once it gets out and other countries know we have a breeding ground, the choice could be made for him."

"Forward your findings to Lange, and I will call him now. I'll talk to you when you get here." Edward hung up. He prepared to call Director Lange, but before he did, he placed one more call to his wife to make sure she was on the road.

◇◇◇◇

Like a pro, Andy flipped through the channels of the television, fast and furiously. Change, change, change, pause … nothing.

What was going on?

He found a news station and left it on. His eyes shifted to the television and to the segment on the President celebrating Christmas Eve.

He walked over to the computer and went on the internet. Something had to be there.

Buzz.

He was hovering over the computer when Chad walked in.

"You look like a man on a mission," Chad said.

"I … I am." Andy stood. He held up a finger, took a moment, and then spoke. "H-h-have you watched the n-n-news?"

"Unfortunately, yes I have. It's frustrating."

"The virus … is o-o-only a blip. Is it d … d-done?"

"No, not at all. Steady at eight states today, but after the holiday, I don't think that will hold. The world, Mr. Jenkins, doesn't stop for much. It stops for Christmas," Chad said. "Despite our recommendations, air travel has not been suspended. They only increased awareness at the airports. That is not going to help. People believe they got their flu shots, they are infallible."

Andy shook his head.

"I think after Christmas this will really break, especially … in light of things. We are actively red. We've sealed this facility until the threat of the pandemic is over or time runs out. I'm going to quote you from your Ice Age book. Civilizations and empires died because of stupidity."

"I ... I … have said th … that a lot."

"I bet. Well, not shutting down air travel is stupid. I suspect that will change. We are burning out Hartworth."

Andy tilted his head. "Ex ... explain."

"The virus is heat resistant. So in order to kill it, we have to burn it and radiate it. Unfortunately, this was a weapon, and the source is still alive and breeding in Hartworth."

Andy's head lowered and he closed his. "L … Lincoln?"

"The weapon will be positioned over Hartworth; that town will be flattened as well."

"What … size?"

Chad squinted his eyes and conveyed a look of curiosity. "15 kiloton. Small by standards but enough to do the job. No one is alive there, Mr. Jenkins. No worries."

Andy nodded. "T...target Har … Har …."

"Hartworth, yes. Airburst. Yes. Hand delivered."

Again, Andy nodded and exhaled.

"Why do you have a look of relief?"

"J-Just worried."

"I see. Anyhow, your seal is lifted. You are free to move about the facility. We have a late pool game starting at ten. You're welcome to join us. We're having pizza."

"Th ... thank you."

"Did you take the meds I gave you?"

Andy nodded.

"Good. They'll take about a week to kick in. You had a head injury, so I am confident in their ability. Then after, we'll talk. I have a lot of questions. Dr. Neil and I both are curious about some things and we're hoping you can share your story."

Andy forced a closed mouth smile and pointed to the computer. "I … st … st … started writing it." He twitched his head. "I … wr … wrote a lot-lot."

"Send it to me, please?" Chad walked to the desk, grabbed a pen, and wrote his email address. "Please. I'm curious, and we can discuss it further later on."

"Yes."

"Excellent. I'll leave you be. See you at pool?" Chad walked to the door.

"May … maybe."

After a nod, Chad left.

Andy settled at the computer, pulled the file, and emailed it immediately to Chad. Then following that, while he still had internet, Andy researched nuclear explosions.

◇◇◇◇

'Emmett Morgan staggered into the street. He was an old man and he waved his hand as best he could as he called out my name for help.

"Andy. Andy, that you?'

Chad read to Edward through the intercom. He read what Andy had written.

'It was obvious that he was sick. He could barely move. I just parked my truck in front of the diner. I wanted to get to my apartment, get my gun, and head to

Hartworth. There were people there I knew. People I cared about. People I had to find.

I wanted to go to him, and I debated it. One more moment in Lincoln could cost me. Already I had walked away from someone I loved to help another. I walked away, never fully comprehending that I could possibly never see this woman again.

I wanted to see the other people, hope that they were alive, but Emmett called for me.

I did the best I could. I helped him back to his house, gave him water, and helped him back into bed. He was strong, very strong, but the sickness was destroying him. He had scratched his belly so badly that I could see tendons.

The sickness eats through the skin like acid. Moreover, it drives them mad. I saw that.

It was when I tried to make Emmet more comfortable that he said something to me. He said, "Andy, don't let me rot right here. Don't let me be forgotten."

I didn't understand that until I left his house.

After I left Emmett, I went to a few other houses. Emmett was one of four people alive. To be in that situation, to see that is a nightmare. It's like a movie, you wait for the ending. Everyone I knew and loved was dead.

I drove to Hartworth; I specifically went to find people I knew, people whose whereabouts I wasn't sure of.

But all I found was death.

I saw the makeshift hospital at the fire hall, and I knew when I walked in there, those people hadn't died from the virus. I saw the bodies that died from the virus. The people in the fire hall weren't all black. The heater was blasting; I shut it down and opened the doors.

I noticed that every one of those people in there had a bracelet with their name on it.

That's when I realized that they would not be forgotten. One day, someone would find the town, would find the bodies, and the people that did would have to figure out who was who.

I didn't know all the people in Hartworth, but I knew a lot. So I went house to house of the folks I knew; I loaded their bodies in the truck, took them to the fire hall, and put one of the bracelets on each of them. They wouldn't be forgotten. Someone would know their names.

I went back to Lincoln. I wanted to come up with a plan for my town. I had lived there all my life. I knew all four hundred people there. When I was in my apartment, I saw all the toys we bought for the baby.

The presents.

The ring I got for her. It wasn't much, but she would never want much.

All I wanted was to spend the rest of my life with her.

That killed me. It killed me because we were planning on the best Christmas ever.

But there wouldn't be a Christmas. For me, there'd never be a Christmas again. I took care and pride in hanging the decorations around town on Black Friday, and I tore them all down that night. Every light, every tree, every bit of tinsel.

While I did that, I came up with a plan of what to do for my town and the people that lived and died there.

"That's as far as he got," Chad said. "We'll get more."

"So the mystery of how the bodies got into the fire hall is now solved," Edward stated.

"Yes. He brought the ones he knew in there and tagged them."

"But one question isn't answered," Edward said.

On that, Chad turned. The door behind him opened, and Andy walked in.

"Andy," Edward spoke. "We were just going over your story."

Chad said, "I asked Andy to come here so we can ask him the question, because it's not in here."

"Wh ... what?" Andy asked.

Edward had the honors. "Andy, on the night of the twentieth, you would have been at the Burton home, correct?"

"Yes."

"A phone call was placed to you. You were the last person to receive a call from Hartworth. What was said?" Edward questioned.

"Goodbye," Andy said. "He … called to say ... say good b-bye."

Chad looked at Edward then to Andy. "It was Lawrence Meadows. The sheriff. Why would he call you?"

"He ... he said he d-did something. D-didn't say wh ... what. He was f-finished. And good … goodbye."

Chad gave a look to Edward. "Bet that was the fire hall cleansing. Andy … but why you? Why did he call you?"

"He ... he's my ... uncle."

Chad immediately jumped to his feet. "Your uncle didn't have the virus."

"I … kn… know. I saw. He k-killed himself."

"So we either have a family immunity or …" Chad stated. "Take off your shirt."

After a curious look and with some hesitation, Andy did.

Chad looked at his shoulder. It was there, the black scar. "Your uncle had this same one."

Andy nodded. "My g-g-grandfather, too. It was a sp-special t-tetanus shot we all g-got."

"Doctor Paltrov?" Chad asked.

Andy nodded.

"This isn't a special tetanus shot, Andy. He gave you an inoculation to this virus. You, your uncle, and your grandfather. The doctor inoculated you. That's why you didn't get sick. You had the vaccine."

Andy looked confused as pulled on his shirt.

"This means," Chad explained, "if you and your uncle didn't get sick, then there is a viable vaccine recipe out there somewhere. And we can stop this thing. We have a shot."

"We just have to find it," Edward added. "Before it's too late."

Chapter Fifteen
Atlanta, GA

December 26th

"Sorry about this," Edward said as he wrote on the final tube of blood.

"No, th… that's fine." Andy pulled down his sleeve. "Take what you n-need. Glad to help."

"I know you are; at least some one is."

Andy stood. "No word?"

Andy shook his head. "Chad's been on the phone with our director. The President had no luck. This afternoon is the day, you know. When we level Hartworth, things will heat up all over. No one is taking the virus seriously, yet we're losing 98% of those infected. This time next week won't be good. Air travel should be suspended. Hopefully."

"V-vaccine?"

"Soviets are denying adamantly that they had any part in this, even though it is highly publicized that they did. Right now, we're trying to find Paltrov's colleagues. Something. I'm thinking, though, if this goes global, which it will because air travel wasn't suspended over the holiday, then we'll hear about a vaccine. Probably the former Soviet Union will emerge with a cure that they 'supposedly' just came up with. By the way … the Pagoclone is working wonders on that stutter. Fast too."

Andy nodded. "The more c-confident I was, the less I st-stuttered. But it is like when I got high or sang, it completely l-left. So I expected it to be fast."

"Another day that may be close to nonexistent."

"Until I run out."

"Just smoke weed."

"I would have. But I w-worked for the city. They d-drug tested." Andy shrugged.

"You don't have that worry anymore. We're kind of hoping that if we don't hear from the Russians regarding a vaccine, then maybe we can create something by watching your blood. Problem is, that takes time. If this moves too fast, then creating a vaccine will be in vain."

"Not really," Andy said. "Even if it t … takes a lot of the population, there will be p-people who were smart. Like your wife. P-people who stayed away from others who will need it to in-integrate back into the world."

"That's true." Edward nodded. "Sort of like what you said in your book, about civilizations dying out because of stupidity. If the world hits an extinction level pandemic, it's only stupidity that caused it, and the smart survive. I was …" He paused when he saw the crinkled nose look on Andy's face. "What's wrong?"

Andy shook his head. "Thought I heard someone."

Chad walked in.

Edward smiled. "I guess you did hear someone."

"So," Chad spoke as he entered. "How is our resident blood machine doing?"

"Fine." Andy replied. "Take as much as you need."

Chad grinned. "How do you feel about that medication? Giving you more confidence? It's working wonderfully."

"Very h-happy. An occasional skip. Better than when I smoked weed."

"Oh. Well, I have some if you want to test the combination."

Andy tilted his head, conveying that it wasn't a bad suggestion

Edward immediately shot a stern look to Andy. "Excuse me?"

Andy cleared his throat and shook his head. "No. But thanks."

"I'm sure," Chad said. "The reason I am here isn't just to see how your veins are holding up. We had a survivor in Hartworth. We hadn't mentioned him by name to you, and this was for the purpose of privacy. Nor did we mention you by name to him. I think you two may know each other or know the same people. It may be good for the grieving process to talk to each other. We'll be down here quite some time." He reached back and looked out the open door, waving his hand. "Come on in."

Edward saw it. The 'throw back' head reaction given by Andy followed by a groan when Del walked in.

"You have to be shitting me," Del said. "Him. He's the sole survivor of Lincoln?" He stepped to Andy. "How's the s-s-stutter."

"G-g-gone." Andy replied.

"What happened to my Emma, Cody …"

"They're no longer with us."

Del huffed out emotionally. "So you're in charge of my family and you failed them."

"I didn't fail them," Andy argued.

"You let them die."

"I did not let them die!" Andy yelled. "Things happened. Things out of our control."

"They were my family."

"You lost your right to call them your family the day you walked out the door," Andy said. "Where were you if you were all that concerned?"

Chad interjected. "He's not immune; he just lucked out. He was arrested."

"I was shot," Del said.

Chad shook his head and spoke nonchalantly. "Minor flesh wound. Nothing to write home about."

"So you hid?" Andy asked.

"I had no choice," Del snapped. "I was trapped. You, on the other hand, had a choice and the ability to do something."

"Bull, I lost my choice and ability the second I watched your daughter die."

"You're an asshole," Del remarked harshly. "Really. Go ahead, lose the stutter, but you're still the big town retard who can't do anything. Who can't protect an innocent baby."

Andy closed his eyes.

"You know …" Chad said in a singing manner.

"Chad," Edward warned.

Chad held up his hand to Edward. "You know, Andy, you're the much bigger guy. I don't understand why you let him speak to you like that. I'd deck him. But that's just me."

Edward saw the widest grin strike Andy's face as he turned his head slowly to look at Chad.

"Someone else once said that to me," Andy said.

Del held out his hands. "What the hell, Dr. Walker?"

"Del?" Andy called his name.

"What?"

Andy decked him. Probably not as hard as he could have, but he nailed him anyhow, sending him spinning down to the floor. He walked to him, flipped him over, and grabbed him by the collar. "That was for Emma. Out of everyone, you don't deserve to live. Not you. You selfish piece of sh … sh… crap." Andy dropped him and walked out.

Chad cleared his throat. "Was it just me, or was there a lot of hostility between the two men?"

Edward grumbled, commented on how it was going to be a long lock down, and pulled Del to his feet.

◇◇◇◇

Andy didn't want to be bothered. As he stretched on the bed, he stared at the photo of Emma, grateful she had printed them. So much was in a digital world; Andy supposed that if technology shut down, so many memories would be lost.

The photo was sealed in a bag.

Edward knocked and then walked in. "How's it going?"

Andy shrugged.

"So … wanna tell me what that was all about?"

"I'm sorry."

"You seem so passive. I am shocked. You hit him good," Edward said.

"Not my best. If... if you want to kick me out. You c-can."

Edward shook his head "Even if I wanted to, I can't. We're on lock down. What's the story?"

"He's the ex of the woman I was involved with. The father of her k-kids. He left a long time ago and popped back up. I g-guess it was just building."

"Wow, so out of all the people, the ex-husband survived?"

Andy cracked a partial smile.

"Can you try to get along? You both have loved and lost the same people. Make it work for you instead of against."

"I'll try." Andy kept his stare on the picture.

"What's that?"

Andy handed it to him.

"Is this the woman you were involved with? She's... beautiful."

"In every way," Andy said sadly. "It's all I have. It got dropped."

"What do you mean?" Edward asked.

"When the sickness started, she made this b-box. In it were pictures of her life. A notebook of her history. She wanted it to remain in c-case, she didn't. So someone c-could find it in the f-future. And know her. This was on the floor."

"That was very smart. The box was left behind?"

Andy nodded.

"I'm sorry. I know it's not there now."

Quickly Andy looked at him. "It's fine. The bomb went off over Hartworth. I saw … saw Lincoln on the news. It's f-flattened, but I know it's safe. It's there."

"You seem very certain."

"I am. When something means so much, you have to believe it's okay. When I get out, I am going to get it. Trust me …" Andy returned to staring at the picture. "Nothing is stopping me from going back to Lincoln."

◇◇◇◇

"Knock, knock," Chad called out from the other side of Del's door.

"Great," Del grumbled and opened it. "Hey, Dr. Walker."

"Chad. Call me Chad. Thank you. I'll come in." He stepped into the room. "How do you like your new accommodations?"

"Better than the hospital-style room."

"How's the cheek?"

Del touched his bruise. "Not too bad. Sore, but I have taken worse."

"It surprised me too how he just seemed to tap you. I expected more."

"And what happened to that stutter?" Del said.

"Well," Chad explained. "The emotional trauma of watching everyone he loved die snapped it right out of him."

"I didn't know that could happen."

"It can't. I'm joking. He's on medication."

Del shook his head in disgust. "You're an instigator."

"I run this facility, and we are on lock down so I can do whatever I want," Chad said

"Then let me out of here. I don't want to be down here."

"Del, you're not immune. Chances are, up there, you won't be so lucky. And aside from that, it's an automatic lock down. I can't override it. You're not a prisoner; you can still make phone calls and go on the computer."

"I watched the news this morning," Del said. "They said they think it's under control, that after disinfecting Montana, the bug will die out."

Chad nodded. "I heard that, too, and my God, do I want to believe that is right. But Del, Billings was infected. The infection spread across the West Coast. The problem we have is it is highly contagious, and it's just started to spread. Air travel wasn't suspended over the holiday. This time next week, we'll know."

Del looked away then turned back to Chad. "Can this thing do to the world what it did to Hartworth?"

"I hope not. I am hoping for a cure or vaccine. But it isn't the virus that will destroy us, if things fall apart. Your 'town retard' wrote an interesting book on why civilization died out. You should read it."

"Andy? Andy Jenkins wrote a book?"

"Several. He's quite smart; get to know him and you'll see." Chad walked to the door. "And Del, we are here for a while. He's the only one you know. I'd really put forth the effort to make amends and get along. It's for the best. You may need each other when the door to the facility opens."

"Yeah, he may be the only one I know down here, but when the door opens, I have my friends"

Chad nodded. "If this virus takes a worst case scenario route, which is possible, he may not only be the only person you know down here, but the only person you have left in the world. Think about it." Chad walked out.

Del moved to the door and closed it. "It can't be that bad. It can't," he said to himself. Then he grabbed the remote control and turned on the news. "I guess time will tell."

Time Stamp – 1

Andy's Journal

January 2nd

Despite the fact that I have been down here, New Years wasn't much different for me. Except I think I drank a little more. These entries will go into my next book; I'm being optimistic about a world left above to read a book. Of course, no one really read my books when there wasn't an epidemic.

For us down here, it was calm. There are only about 25 of us. I believe this facility was built for fifty or more. The recreation room is nice, but I keep mainly to myself. I make it a point to say hello to Del. I'm trying. We have a long time down here ahead of us. He doesn't speak much to anyone either, but that isn't a social thing, it's more of him watching the news constantly. It's always on in his room, plus he is constantly on the 'net connecting, warning, getting the truth out.

It's started. Some people right now are paying attention. New Year's Day started off with a bang, literally. Half the world condemned our President for using a nuclear weapon on our own soil; the others more than just condemned, they threatened. He did what he had to do, and I felt bad watching him defend his actions.

People insist that Lincoln, Hartworth, and Mead weren't really wiped out by a virus, but rather there was an attack or the US was weapons testing. Conspiracy theories gone mad. Weren't they paying attention to what was happening in Los Angeles or Seattle, the scores of people not only getting sick, but also dying?

As of today, air travel has not been suspended. They use these heat scanners, because fever is a big first symptom. People with any cold symptoms are not permitted to board. Nevertheless, this is all going to contribute to an outbreak that will be far from controlled in a month's time. I can't see how it won't. The symptoms hit you in the snap of the fingers. On just one flight from LA to New York, a person can develop symptoms. It's happened. They already quarantined a plane in Cleveland.

Dr. Walker told me the CDC estimates that only 8% of the population is getting the virus. Day eighteen of the virus since release in Hartworth and 8%. No one is worried about 8%; they should be. Eight percent of the United States' population is thirty million people. It has a kill rate of nearly 100%.

That means thirty million people don't go to work or to school. Who is doing their jobs?

Last week it was less than 1% with the virus, this week 8%. Next week? Who knows?

When will people stop being stupid? When will they suspend air travel and do everything possible to stop this thing from spreading? Shut down schools, initiate a 'necessary jobs only' rule. Keep people in their homes and allow this thing to burn out and infect as few as possible.

I'm afraid by the time these steps are taken, it will be too late.

However, I am not an expert.

Right now, like Del, I am just an observer.

He observes the television and I watch the countdown timer above the facility door.

I have 153 days remaining. I feel I'll be here that entire time.

Time Stamp – 2

Andy's Journal

January 22nd

Ed is working extremely hard on the virus. He was discouraged again by no news from the former Soviet Union regarding the vaccine. They publicly insisted the other day that Ebolapox was an invention of the United States, and they refuse to take credit for such a horrendously inhumane virus.

Well, someone created it, and someone has the vaccine.

I think Ed is working hard for his family. He called them frantically today because the workers that went to Hartworth with him are now sick. Those people worked with him daily. His family is fine; he wants to keep them that way. His goal is to bring them a vaccine when the seal opens. I understand that.

A woman named Martha has vowed to document her illness every single hour and work until she cannot work anymore. She won't work for long.

Del said the virus is still not always headline news, and other things take precedence. How ridiculous. North Korea, South Korea, who cares. It will be moot if this virus takes hold.

Dr. Walker, or Chad, seems optimistic. He says it is nearing being contained despite air travel continuing.

Day 38 of the virus – 16% of population infected. No Cure. Kill rate 99.9%

133 days remain inside the facility.

Time Stamp – 3

Andy's Journal

January 27th

I do and I don't understand humanity. On one hand, I get why people fight for survival; on the other I don't get why they don't fight instead, to stay alive as a whole. Who wants to destroy someone over a gallon of water, when you can easily save both of you by sharing?

Del was upset when a riot broke out in Los Angeles. It was a huge riot. He heard about it first from his publicist. His publicist hadn't left his house in days. He had stocked up and planned to wait it out.

With typical Del neuroticism and obsession, he put on the news, but nothing was there for at least an hour after Del received the phone call. His publicist Max told Del that the southern part of the city was in flames. Martial law was instituted, and no one was to go out.

Yet on the news, they seemed to focus on that one area. Looting, fighting. I swore I saw the same footage years ago. I swore it, but who knows.

Who in the heck fights over televisions? Why are they out fighting over technology? What do rioting and looting prove? Why turn over police cars and attack people?

The enemy is a virus, not each other.

The incident in Los Angeles prompted the President to take action.

By midnight, the entire continental United States will be under martial law.

Thank God. Maybe with control of people will come control of the virus.

Day 43 of the virus – 19% of the population infected.

128 days to go.

Time Stamp – 4

Andy's Journal

January 29th

This was an insane day, and probably the most I ever watched the news as much as Del. Because I spend so much time with Del, I understand why he lost so much weight. He wasn't all that big to begin with, but he barely eats; when he's not watching the television he's on a conspiracy site.

We're talking more; today really brought that out.

He actually came into my room and woke me. Scared the hell out of me. Told me I had to get up, that there was an emergency meeting of the UN counsel.

The UN pulled all of its delegates out of the United States. Now, really, was that smart? Let's take a bunch of people in the US, a place where every single state now has at least one case of the sickness, and let's send these people back to their countries.

The ever-threatening France, and I say that with sarcasm, gave a harsh warning along with Russia for the United States to control their outbreak or they will.

What the heck is that supposed to mean? Really. If the information is correct, Dr. Paltrov came from Russia and so did the germ.

Come on, people instead of fighting. Cure this thing.

Day 45 of the virus – hanging tight at 19% infected.

126 days to go until freedom.

Time Stamp – 5

Andy's Journal

February 3rd

Del passed out today. He was racing down the hall, no one really knows why, but he just dropped. His body just gave in, and his heart stopped from not eating or drinking enough. They were able to revive him. He's under sedation while they pump him with stuff.

What the heck was he trying to prove? Did he just want to die? I think so. That isn't going to happen, not when I'm around. When he comes to, I am going to yell at him. He was lucky enough to beat the germ, lucky enough to be below while it rages above. After visiting him and waiting for him to wake up, which he didn't, I went back to his room. Thought I'd post on his social media site about his condition.

He was always on there updating; hopefully he left it logged in.

When I got to his room, the television blared as usual, and I saw why he probably was running, trying to do those Del 'updates' when something urgent or new comes on.

The germ broke barriers.

First reported cases in the UK, Spain, and Germany. Guess no one will be telling us to secure our borders.

The estimates went up on how many are ill. Hospitals are overflowing, and FEMA is setting up sick camps, opening up the gates of disaster camps across the nation. Pictures on the television showed people lining up and struggling to get in there.

Didn't they pay attention to the news, the health bulletins? There is no cure. The only thing they can give you is pain medication, and that isn't a sure thing with the numbers stacking. Hell, if I were sick I'd be damned if I were gonna die in some FEMA camp.

I pulled forth Del's computer to update his site. I wanted to see where he left off; instead I think I saw the scariest reality of this germ yet. The news feed came up. Now I'm not a big social media guy, but even with my two hundred friends, that social media news feed was always updated with new posts.

I thought it was an error so I refreshed. There was one or two new status updates in his news feed. The next newest was eight hours earlier.

That wasn't even as scary as the fact that every one of those status updates were about how sick the person was.

Day 50 of the virus – 25% of the population infected.

121 days until the door opens.

Time Stamp – 6

Andy's Journal

February 18th

My conversation with Del could have gone worse. He admitted that he didn't care if he lived or died, because he knew the world he was a part of was no longer going to be there. I told him I went to Hartworth once preparing to find his dead body; I refused to see him die now. He admitted his obsession with being on the social media, watching daily as people posted that they were ill or a family member was ill.

He spent two weeks in that hospital bed. I told him he had to get strong, we'd run up and down the halls if we had to. Use the exercise equipment. I knew I was, because I didn't know if I'd get a car, horse, or have to walk to Montana, but I was going back to Lincoln. I was snatched up from there like some undercover operation.

I need to see, I need to say goodbye, and I need to get to that box that Emma made.

It's funny down here, and I rarely touch upon how life is. When the facility was first sealed, people were quiet, then as it seemed that the virus wasn't taking hold, people were more upbeat.

Now, no one talks. At all. Everyone is kind of down, talking to family members that weren't making it. Most, though, were like myself and didn't have family. I suppose that was why they volunteered.

India believed that found a cure. They sent the so-called recipe our way three days ago, and one of the test subjects volunteered to be injected with the virus to test the cure.

This was not why they were here. They were here to donate blood, tissue samples. Lung lining samples. Not be infected. But Chad saw promise as India did.

They believed it worked only on those just exposed.

The only thing that worked was the fact that the test subject skipped over the cold symptoms that first day, and on the second, he was black. We were all hopeful that he didn't get sick. But then he did.

He died the third day.

He said before he died that he didn't care.

That seems to be the attitude around here lately. I hope the spirit of survival and hope cycles back around. If it doesn't, then us being here is pointless.

We all want it to get better. We all want to wake up and hear on the news that it's over.

However, we are all so close to the science of it that we know that's not happening.

I still pray.

Day 65 of the virus – 28% infected.

106 days remaining until we go above.

Time Stamp – 7

Andy's Journal

February 24th

Thirty-three percent. Yesterday, it was determined that thirty-three percent of the world's population was infected with the virus. It was the biggest jump in percentage we had seen in one week since the onset. Now, let me explain, that is not thirty-three percent of the remaining, that's over all.

The United States is well over forty percent. Already we resolved ourselves to a much emptier world.

Thirty-three percent. That is three billon people dead.

That is not including those who have died from the elements. Starvation is rampant. There is a water crisis. I feel bad eating my M&Ms when children are starving and dying, when people are fighting for every bit of food there is.

Things have finally changed above … according to the news. The news now only talks about the virus. Potential cures, treatments, violence.

Only essential workers are to report to work, and air travel is limited to essential travel of diplomats and emergency health workers.

Doesn't matter. No one flies anymore. No one travels. The positive thing is those who remain healthy are staying inside, not coming out. That's a blessing.

Del and I started jogging around the facility. We increase our laps by one each time the percentage goes up. He's a bit healthier and gaining weight. He has a focus. He's gonna come with me to Montana, and I told him I will not have a weaker party tag along.

Chad says each day that goes by, even though more are infected, he himself is working on a cure.

What the hell happened with Russia? They're infected, too. Did they lose that recipe or did it go by the wayside with the virus?

Chad doesn't talk about his wife. I asked. He said she was fine, and they had a contingency plan. Admittedly, I used to hate asking Ed about his family. Now, he gives me the update. I actually wait every day to hear him say they are doing well.

The news is grim. Even Del stopped watching it as much. Today they showed Los Angeles Stadium. It was burning. But they showed aerial shots before they did. It was packed with people. Sick people. It was so reminiscent of Katrina back in 2005.

But they all died there and they burned the stadium.

The newscasters look tired and beat. I wonder how much longer they'll hold up.

Day 71 of the virus – 33% infected.

100 days left in this place.

Time Stamp – 8

Andy's Journal

March 10th

'While we feel lost, there is still hope. Though we feel deflated, we have not been defeated. We are weary in a battle that has beaten us, but we have not yet lost the war.'

Even though I believe I'll remember those words spoken by the President, I wrote them down. They were powerful and delivered in a message intended to implore us to keep fighting, but in my heart and mind, I saw it no less than a farewell to humanity.

He announced that he was staying above, that he wasn't going into a safe location like other world leaders. It wasn't fair that he should have that advantage when others did not.

How bad was it up there? So much so that he saw no future need for his leadership? Sure, the Vice President went in his place. But still.

It was sobering and real.

I wished I didn't watch it. I'm really off today.

This is the first time I truly felt the end was nigh.

Perhaps it is.

Day 85 of the virus – 48% infected.

86 days remaining.

Time Stamp – 9

Andy's Journal

March 22nd

The President came on the news; his wife and daughter passed away. He didn't look good. Maybe he should have gone into a safe location.

Rolling power outages due to lack of employees caused the news to be sporadic and only hourly until eleven p.m. I caught a segment on body disposal. The federal government was no longer responsible for bodies. There was very little news about other countries on the stations. I guess everyone worried about themselves.

The newscaster spoke while handy dandy tips on what to do with decreased family members scrolled the screen as if they were directions to baking a cake.

Each community was responsible for their own body landfill.

Each family was responsible for their own deceased. They had to prep the body, wrap it, and bring it to the landfill.

It was odd because I saw a similar scene in a Vincent Price movie, an old black and white movie that was later redone with Charlton Heston. I remember Vincent Price's character carrying his wife or daughter to the landfill and rolling her over the hill where a perpetual fire burned. Workers kept the flames going as if it were some steel mill.

From the station wagon to the pit. His heart broke. He wanted to roll down that hill and join her. The world was void of caring people. No one really cared when the world around them died.

I suppose that was happening now.

I remember seeing that film and thinking that they were far off, that would never happen. It was happening. Like in the movie, so many were dying there weren't enough left to bury the dead.

When it is all said and done, and I pray there are still many left, I believe there will be too many bodies to remove. I believe cities will be torn down, burned. Forgotten. All those people who lived lives, dreamed, and loved would never be any more than a statistic.

Over dinner, Del expressed concern over the lack of news. What would happen when it stopped? How would we know what to expect when we emerged?

We run on generator power, and above us are cameras. We can watch the lobby, outside the center, and a little of the street. I declined watching.

The news is reality enough. I didn't need to see the world outside.

I wasn't ready.

Day 97 of the virus – 55% infected

64 days until I am forced to see what lies above.

Time Stamp – 10

Andy's Journal

April 3rd

The United States sits at the highest infection rate. Russia is rapidly catching up. We never heard anything from them regarding a vaccine. China, however, seems to have pulled through. From their underground 'doomsday' lab, they seem to have cracked the code. They believe they have what they are calling the morning after vaccine. It works before exposure and within twenty-four hours of exposure. They started testing.

Phone contact isn't guaranteed; Chad is hoping for results soon. Chad could create the vaccine and test it down here, but even if it worked, there was no way to produce more than a hundred doses here in the facility.

A hundred doses was really nothing.

China and India were still on the low end of the infection rate. They told Chad that if the vaccine proved successful, they would inoculate all those within the facility and go topside by overriding the seal. China could do that. We could not.

Even if we could, the United States didn't have the resources or the bodies to mass produce the serum. We lost all power two days ago. While we still had generators, the rest of the US lives in the dark.

China's plan was to mass-produce the serum with help from India and Japan. However, best-case scenario was three months, realistically six.

A little too late for this side of the world.

Day 108 of the virus – 68% infected.

53 days left until the seal is broken.

Time Stamp – 11

Andy's Journal

April 30th

It took Chad Walker nearly two weeks to copy the serum successfully. He refused to believe, despite what the Chinese had told him, that it worked, and then he ran simple lab tests. It looked promising.

China had informed him they had already moved into mass production.

They had power, they had news, and we had dark.

Five days ago, four people volunteered to be test subjects. Two would get the vaccine before exposure, two after.

Del was one of those people. I was so angry. He and I just actually started to become friends and he did that.

It angered me that his reasoning was weak. He owed it to nobody to be a guinea pig, but he did anyhow.

I spent the days watching the surveillance. Everybody did at one time or another. Eight monitors and someone always caught something.

At first, there were many people coming in and out of the CDC. They weren't workers. Somewhere in everything that happened, Chad and Edward failed to tell us the CDC closed down. We learned that when we saw the broken glass.

People were desperate, looking for things.

Fires burned; we could see them better at night.

Every once in a while, someone would point out movement.

Was that a person? I think so, yes.

Del survived the testing. The serum worked both as a vaccine and as morning-after treatment. It was a shallow victory, but Edward was happy. He spoke to his wife and believed it was the last time he'd speak to her until he went to their safe house.

Her generator power was fading and the phones would be out of commission.

They were still healthy, and Edward wanted to deliver the vaccine himself.

The woman that cooks our meals gave a lot of us haircuts. It passed the time and prepped us for the world in our final days in the facility.

Chad began working on producing doses of the serum. He'd give it to everyone in the shelter and extra to those who needed to take it to family members they knew were alive.

Last, we spoke to China; they insisted they would drop vaccines once they provided for their own.

Would it even matter?

Day 135 of the virus – 72% infected.

26 days to go.

Time Stamp – 12

Andy's Journal

May 24th

This is my last entry in the journal. I am now packing what few things I have in a survivor backpack to take with me on my journey.

I have no idea how Del and I will get to Montana, but we will. We will.

Edward will find his wife, and Chad said he was confident his wife went into the house's safe room. He designed it for such an event. It was the first he spoke of his wife the entire time here, at least to me.

There is nothing left up there, at least in Atlanta. The last movement we saw on the street was ten days ago.

We watch. Every day, diligently we watch for any speck of movement. Even a rat. Nothing. I wonder what waits for us above. It has been so long since I saw the sun, felt the warmth. It was snowing when I came down here.

We will emerge to a completely dead world. Will it be violent? Will those who survived this plague of horror be shells of human beings caring less for each other, or did they band together as survivors, making communities?

Did the Vice President come out of hiding, rally the troops, and start things? We don't know. We lost all ability to communicate with anyone.

We may have lights, but we are in the dark.

The doses are done, sealed, and packed. But it doesn't matter. Maybe it does, just as a safeguard against future infections.

But when the timer counts down and the door opens, we will walk into a world that is safe from infection. Not because the infection was cured, but because every person that was to get sick … got sick. Every person that was to die has died.

There are no more hosts to spread the virus.

God help us all, and I pray, I just pray all is not lost.

Day 159 of the virus – we stopped keeping track of the infected.

Two more days left.

THE EMERGING

Chapter Sixteen

May 26th

Like school children waiting for recess, they lined up in front of the only exit door that was viable. The clock counted down.

Edward seemed the most enthusiastic, waiting to go to find his family. It was a six-hour drive that he hoped to begin right away. He had to go first; he had gasoline stored at the house.

If, of course, the house was still there.

Andy stood with Del and carried a small pack over his shoulder. It was from Chad.

"There are sixty more days of the medication in there," Chad told Andy. "After that I can't guarantee if the stutter will come back or if you'll be able to get more. Perhaps you'll be lucky and find some marijuana."

"Doesn't matter," Andy replied. "I'll deal." He was excited. His stomach twitched in hopefulness and fear, and then the counter reached zero.

The buzz went through him like an electric shock. There was a hiss as Edward reached for the door. It opened.

The journey topside was no less than eighteen flights of stairs, a marathon of exercise Del and Andy were more than ready for.

The others were not. They stammered and stopped, rested, then moved. Andy and Del ended up leading the way. The staircase led to the far end of the employee-parking garage. That was where Edward hoped the car would be, a car left there by Martha.

Andy wasn't even winded when he reached the top, Del right at his side. He looked over the banister and hollered down. "I'm gonna go check it out. Stay put. We just don't know." He then turned to Del and told him to hang tight, and Andy alone opened that final door.

There was a spring smell to the air, and it wasn't what Andy expected. He prepared for a raw smell, death, maybe even burning. But nothing.

The dead had passed on long enough beforehand that they left no smell.

Dust was thick on the remaining cars in the lot. He ran his fingers across them as he raced toward the sunlit entrance of the garage.

Already, before he even arrived, the daylight hurt his eyes. He took a few steps, paused, moved, and paused.

Inching his way into the sun, Andy let his eyes adjust. They watered and burned; soon the blurry vision left, and he stepped into the street.

It wasn't a wise move because Andy didn't know what awaited them.

Nothing.

Empty streets, quiet like he had never experienced. Not a bird, animal … nothing.

"Hello!" he called out loudly.

His voice echoed back.

He tried again. "Hello!"

Not a roll of a can, a scuffle of movement, only silence. The sky was blue, the early morning sun was bright and the temperature warm. Andy went back to the garage.

It was time to tell the others they could come out; there was no danger because there was nothing.

◇◇◇◇

Edward kept the battery as charged as he could in the facility and was able to start the car with ease. After it charged some, he jump-started other cars. He was the first of all to pull out. Andy drove, because Edward's eyes were having trouble adjusting.

Andy and Del said their goodbyes to Chad, and promised to return or find a way to contact him.

Chad had no idea where he'd end up, but he said he'd leave word at his home and gave Andy and Del the address.

Edward didn't want to waste the gas to drive Andy and Del to the outskirts of Atlanta. They would try to find a vehicle outside of town; if unable to do so, they'd walk.

Andy was certain they'd find transportation eventually. Many people died. Many cars were left and gas buried in the ground at defunct fueling stations.

"Are you sure you don't want to go to Virginia with me?" Edward asked. "It's wonderful property." Andy shook his head. "No, I have to go to Lincoln. I left something there I have to get."

"Nothing is left," Edward told him.

"I'm certain that this is left," Andy said.

"Del?" Edward asked.

"I go where he goes. As much as we hated each other, he's all I got."

Edward nodded, and then he wished them good luck.

Andy and Del began their journey. They had food and water and would ration as best as they could. They walked all morning and into the afternoon.

Somewhere around three, a pickup truck stopped and asked them if they needed a ride. It was the first vehicle Andy had seen all day.

When the older man asked where they were going, he laughed at the response of Montana.

He told Andy and Del he would take them as far as Alexandria, Virginia, but that was where he stopped.

They accepted and got in the truck.

Their first run-in with a survivor was good, and Andy hoped it would be an informative trip.

◇◇◇◇

Chad was quiet on the ride to his house. Carl, who lived in an apartment building nearby, drove Chad to his home.

Atlanta's downtown was desolate, but it wasn't completely devoid of people. They saw a few, but not many as they left the confines of the city.

Chad's neighborhood was upscale, and he knew as soon as he turned onto his street that looters had already hit the neighborhood.

Houses were burned, windows broken, belongings strewn into the street.

Chad's was not immune. His front door was open, his couch on the front lawn.

"Maybe I should go in with you," Carl said.

"No, wait here. Can you?" Chad asked. "I want to check the safe room."

Carl nodded.

"Hopefully, if she isn't there, she left a note or something." Chad stepped from the car and walked the path to his home.

It had been vandalized, pictures knocked form the wall, papers everywhere. At first glance, he could see that every drawer was open. They came for food. Chad walked up the stairs.

There was an odd smell to his house. Musty, sour, but it wasn't a fresh smell. Chad's gut rang with instinct that something was wrong.

The safe room was located at the back of the master bedroom closet, but Chad didn't need to go into the safe room to find Belinda.

She didn't go into the safe room at all.

Her body was so decomposed that it was evident she had been dead for months. It also was clear she didn't die of the plague. A portion of her head was missing. A huge brown stain of blood formed a halo around the saturated pillow, and the gun was still in her hand.

She had taken her own life.

He had some sense of sadness, but a part of him knew. When he hadn't spoken to her and she hadn't answered the phone, he knew. He'd hoped she had gone into the safe room.

Chad covered her, took a moment, said goodbye, and then he gathered a few pictures from the home, some clothes, and he left.

◇◇◇◇

Rollin, Virginia

Edward used the last five-gallon can of gas just before he turned up the mountain road. That was it; that was all he had. The only redeeming feature was the small town ten miles before. He saw a few people there and a sign that said 'gas for food'.

Edward had that and something more valuable. The cure.

The plan was his wife and children, along with Edward's mother, would go to the house, a cottage deep in the hills and stocked with a year's supply of food and well water.

It was far enough away from civilization that as long as his wife and children left before exposure and stayed away they would be safe.

He would be lying to himself if he thought for sure everything was fine. Truth was, Edward was scared. Scared to death that he'd arrive and find his entire family dead.

The road was overgrown, and the last mile was quiet.

He pulled through the open gate and saw the SUV parked into front of the house. It was 'weather' dirty, and weeds grew up almost to the tires. The car hadn't been moved or touched.

The curtains were drawn; there were no signs of life.

It was a beautiful day; surely, the children would be out playing.

Edward turned off the car and paused for a moment. He prayed and then gathered the courage to go to the house. The step creaked as he placed his foot on it. He didn't want to call out because he didn't want silence to be the answer.

Edward reached for the door. Before he even touched the knob, the door opened and his wife Donna gasped out.

He couldn't take it all in as his children cried out, "Daddy," and grabbed on to his legs as he grabbed his wife.

He didn't think beyond that moment. Edward hadn't a clue what the next step would be. He'd think about it... later. For that moment, he was happy. His family was alive and well and that was all that mattered to Edward.

◇◇◇◇

Alexandria, VA

The pickup truck driver was a nice enough fellow to Andy. More than being nice, he was informative to Andy and Del on the five-hour trip.

His name was Ben, and he was from Sarasota, Florida, one of the last places in the United States to be hit with the Black Hartworth, the name they gave to the germ that swept the country and eventually the world.

Andy loved the information Ben provided. Ben lost his entire family, except an uncle to the Black Hartworth. He said people fled the West Coast and unfortunately brought the virus, and then they came south. They lost the news, then the internet, then the power. Radio was still operational two hours a day through FEMA broadcasting networks.

Even though Andy and Del had a radio in the facility, being so far underground made it worthless. So no one in the CDC facility heard the FEMA broadcast.

News came that China had a cure, but it was going to take months.

"Gotta understand," Ben told them, "This China Cure thing came at the end, when people were desperate and worn. That's when the Atlanta riot began. People stormed the CDC, and then things kind of just … fizzled."

Ben explained that the United States, like every other country, lost its sustainability and structure. Forget financial. That all went by the wayside. Everyone concentrated on rebuilding, sustaining life, and then reconnecting.

According to President Wallace, the former Vice President, the order of importance was food and water, shelter, healthcare, power, communications, security, and finances.

The restructuring of sustainability was set to begin on June 1.

There were nine government contract hubs. People were urged to register for work. They'd be fed, transported, and cared for in exchange for useful skills.

Ben worked for the power company for eight years. He got the power back up in Sarasota and was certain that was where his skills would be needed.

When they pulled into Alexandria, there were droves of people, men and women, carrying belongings, standing in line.

"This is insane," Del said. "I did not expect this many people."

"This is just one of the sign-up places. People need food. This country needs farmers, teachers, and workers. You name it, the sustainability project will do it. We hope. At the very least it'll bring people together."

Andy gave an up nod of his head. "I didn't expect to see soldiers."

"A lot went into the safe location with the Vice President," Ben replied. "They divided them between hubs. They still need people to patrol streets. That's on the list as well. You two ought to join."

Andy nodded. "I will, but I have to get back to Montana first."

Ben laughed. "Here I thought that was a joke. Even though there is gas in the reserves, it's rationed. You can catch a ride to the next hub. Maybe there you can request gas to go to the hub farthest west."

"That's sounds like a good idea. Del?" Andy called his attention.

"All these people. Somehow I didn't think this many would survive."

Ben stated, "They estimate a little under twenty percent. But still, twenty percent, that's seventy million people. That's as many people as there were in 1880. At least that's what the radio said."

Ben pulled over and parked. He wanted to get his place in line, and Andy and Del had to part ways with him.

The sign up station was on the outskirts of Alexandria in a ballpark parking lot. Del was recognized by one of the soldiers and able to get a ride. He told the solider they needed to go west.

The soldier found them transportation. They could ride with the truck, but it didn't leave until morning. They'd get out west, but it would take a while.

That was fine with them.

Andy and Del didn't stray from where they'd catch their ride. They had enough supplies. To Andy it didn't matter how long it would take; he was below for over five months and away from Lincoln, what was a few more days?

Chapter Seventeen

May 30th

Lincoln, Montana

"There's nothing out there. It's Babylon. Everyone left," a soldier told them. "It's barren."

"It's home," Del simply responded.

It was a roundabout way and took a lot of explaining, but finally, they made it to Montana from one Sustainability Project hub to the next, Louisville, Cincinnati, Chicago, and Twin Falls. From there they finally got a truck.

But everyone was right.

The last sign of life they saw was in a little town called Bookings, South Dakota. The empty Holiday Inn even had on their marquee, last stop for civilization.

Not a soul. Not a car. Every town they drove through was empty. But just as they crossed out of Garfield County in Phillips, the road ended … literally.

Dirt and dust covered the highway. There were some trees, but not many.

There was no point of direction, nothing. They moved on a hope and a prayer; Andy prayed the entire way.

It wasn't what he expected.

He followed the news. The small nuclear warhead was detonated over Hartworth.

They were forty miles from Hartworth. Were they wrong? Did the news mislead? Was the bomb bigger, or was there more than one?

"This looks worse than the pictures of Hiroshima," Del commented. "You aren't finding that box, Andy."

"I have to try."

Del exhaled with a nod.

Driving was tedious, like a video game. Some of the road lifted, some was just gone, but the sign that read 'Lincoln, Montana', was a godsend. It was bent and dirty, but still half in the ground, and Andy knew he was home.

He knew right where he was even though there weren't any other visual markers. He had lived in that area his entire life; he was certain that he could find the Burton property.

Skeletons of horses scattered about and an RV lay on its side, dented and dirty. It looked as if it had been thrown.

Andy spotted the hill of Stew's property, the one where his house used to sit, and he turned right, even though the road was gone.

Del kept asking, "Are you sure this is right? Nothing is here."

"It's right," Andy said. "I feel it."

Then they saw the remains of Stew's fence. The tall brick walls that were pillars for the metal gate were still standing as well as the gate. It was open, though.

They arrived on the property.

Typically, Stew's house could be seen on top of the hill, as well as the large barn, but they were gone.

Rubble was strewn across the property, couches, furniture, and clothes tossed about, covered with dirt.

Andy made a turn; it was the road built to Emma's house. He could make out a portion of it, counted in his mind, and estimated where the driveway was.

But he couldn't go very far.

Wood and bricks were everywhere.

Emma's house, her barn, were nothing but matchsticks as if the hand of God crushed the buildings, and tossed out the remains, sprinkling them across the land.

Andy put the truck in park and stepped out. The ache in his body seeped through and he groaned when he closed the door.

Del watched for a moment. Andy was on a mission. He walked a few steps, backed up, turned, and walked again. What was he doing?

He repeated his actions over and over, and then Del had enough. He got out of the truck. "Andy," he called. "Come on, guy. This is useless."

Andy spun to face Del. "It is not useless. I'm not giving up. Not yet."

Del tossed out his hands. "What can I do?"

"Look."

"For?"

"Anything that points to the direction of the house," Andy said.

The search would be defeating and Del knew it. He shook his head, but when he did, he saw it. "Like that step?"

Andy stopped.

The step was twenty feet west of where Andy looked.

He rushed to it. "Yes. Yes, Del." Andy removed planks of wood. "This is the steps to the porch." Andy walked up.

Del watched as Andy stepped over the rubble, reached out his hand, and pretended to open a door. "You look insane, you know that, right?"

"I'm in the living room." Andy said and turned. "Headed to the kitchen now."

"He's in the living room."

"Del! Come on. I need your help."

"Why not?" Thinking that Andy had lost it, but what else was there to do, they had come all this way, Del walked through the rubble to join Andy.

Andy moved frantically, tossing planks of wood, stomping his boot, then lifting some more. "It's here."

"The box?"

"The basement. Listen." Andy tromped. "Hollow. This wood is blocking it."

"The box is in the basement?" Del asked.

"Sort of." Andy moved more determined, tossing the wood as if it weighed nothing, ignoring the cuts that formed on his hands. Finally, he broke through. After lifting a piece of linoleum, he exposed a small hole. He pulled forth his backpack, lifted a flashlight, and aimed it in the hole. "That's it."

"You have the basement?" Del asked with a smile.

"Yep. Go to the truck. Get that rope they gave us. Move the truck this way and secure the rope to the bumper in case I get stuck."

Del nodded and took off.

Andy cleared more of the debris, exposing even more of the hole. The more he pulled the more he saw he did indeed find the basement steps.

He heard the truck approach, then Andy stood. "I got the steps. Looks like the basement is intact."

"Do you need the rope?" Del asked.

"Bring it just in case." Andy took the first step. He felt to make sure the staircase was secure, and then he hurried down.

It was there, right there, he saw it across the basement. The white shelf. That part of the basement was so far underground it was protected and intact. However, the shelf was blocked by debris. Just as Andy made it to the shelf, Del entered the basement.

"What are you doing?" Del asked.

Andy started tossing bricks, boards, and other things out of the way from the shelf. "Getting to the door. Help me."

Del joined him.

"There's not a lot," Andy said. "Just push it until the shelf is fully exposed and we can move it." His hands worked as he spoke. He paused occasionally and tried the shelf. If it didn't move, Andy kept working.

"I have to say, Andy, this is a hell of a lot of work just for a box."

Emotionally, winded, Andy looked over his shoulder to Del. "It's more than a box. Much more than a box."

As he worked at freeing the door, Andy thought back.

That last phone call. The one from his Uncle Larry. It wasn't to say goodbye, like Andy told everyone.

"Got an RV full of people, they said you know about them. They aren't sick, Andy. None of them," Larry said. "What do you think we should do?"

"Tell them to drive to the Burton property," Andy told his uncle.

The shelf freed, and Andy moved it, exposing the metal door.

"Is that … is that The Hole?" Del asked.

Andy nodded and reached for the still-lit keypad. He punched in the code.

"Andy, I can't," Emma told him. "I can't. It's been fine in theory. But for real? I can't."

He told her she had to, it was the only way; it had to be done. It was the smart thing to do when civilization would fall apart from stupidity.

The metal door opened.

"Jesus," Del whispered. "She really went all out."

Andy said nothing; he turned on his flashlight, started to race down the twenty-foot hall and, halfway there, he stopped. He froze. His heart broke, and Andy couldn't move. He physically couldn't do anything but drop to the floor.

The box.

The 'history of Emma' box that Emma had made set in the hallway.

"You found the box," Del said. "Oh my God."

Andy shook his head.

"What's wrong?"

'Andy, if I don't make it, if I get sick, I don't want you finding me," Emma had told him. "I'll leave the box in the hall. That is my sign that we didn't make it."

"Andy?" Del questioned.

Andy took a moment, and then he stood. Slowly and emotionally, he stood with that box in his arms. He held his tears, sniffed once, and turned.

Shift.

The sound of a shotgun being pumped caused him to stop.

"Who's there?" the husky male voice called out.

Andy slowly turned around.

"Good God in Heaven, Andy Jenkins, that you?"

Del's flashlight beam lit the man's face. "Mr. Bailey? Holy shit."

Andy dropped the box and raced forward. "Tell me …"

A scream.

A loud, long scream came from the other end of the hall, and out of the darkness raced Emma. Cody in her arms, she ran full speed ahead and slammed right into Andy. Her free arm wrapped around his neck.

Her scream turned into an emotional cry that was deep and heartfelt. "I thought you were dead."

"Oh, God." Andy held her tight, stepped back, and looked at her. "The box. It's in the hall."

Emma shook her head. "When we heard the bombs, we thought …" Another shake of her head. "We were trapped, Andy. We thought we were gonna die down here or be here forever."

"Your girl," Mr. Bailey waved a finger. "Her and her planning. It saved the rest of us."

Andy rested his hand on her face, kissed her and then Cody. "She got big." Andy's eyes lifted. Everyone from the shelter gathered in that hall, led by Richie.

Richie grinned and ran to him.

Andy reached out pulling him into him.

Del cleared his throat. "Um, hello. I'm here, too." He reached out and grabbed hold of Cody. "And I am not letting you out of my sight, little one." Then Del did something else; he signed to Richie. "I'm not letting you out of my sight, either. Get used to it." He embraced his son.

Richie laughed and replied. "You learned to sign?"

Del pointed to Andy. "We've been together."

Emma asked. "This whole time?"

Andy nodded. "CDC had us in lock down while things went bad. They cured my stutter for a spell. We have time to talk about that."

Bailey interjected. "We were able to get a radio signal about two weeks after the bombs were dropped. We lost that a couple weeks ago, thought everyone in the world died."

Del stated. "Not really. But most did. It's a different world up there."

Emma inched to Andy. "How is it up there, Andy? Really?"

"Better now." As best as he could, Andy brought Emma and Cody close to him. He closed his eyes tight and inhaled a warm gratefulness. "Much better now."

Time Stamp – Final

Andy's Journal

September 2nd

I know I had said I wasn't going to write another entry, but I felt the need to add closure to it all.

There were eleven people in The Hole. All of them in good health, good spirits, and their weight was good. Not only did Emma have a ridiculous amount of stock, her hydroponics were unbelievable. Canning and preserving what she grew passed a lot of the time.

The last I spoke to Emma, I had called from her father's house and told her she needed to go into The Hole. It had its own safe air system that filtered for a month. But she was so far out that I didn't think she needed to do that, or she and I would have been infected already.

She didn't have a heads up on Richie's arrival. I knew the inner door would be sealed, but apparently, Emma just let them in. She didn't make them wait it out. According to her, it didn't matter. She took a gamble and it paid off. Incidentally, Del's lady friend and her son never made it to Bailey's RV.

But after the bombs, debris trapped them down there. They were able to retract the outer air pump and use the in-house ventilation. After a radiation readout showed that the air was safe, the design allowed them to drill the pipe upward. The hatch in the barn was completely covered and so was the other exit. The only way out was to redesign my ventilation drill and constantly drill a way out.

Bailey was making some progress when we arrived. They had to be careful, because they used up all the in-house ventilation.

After everyone was out, me, Mr. Bailey and another man headed into Miles City. It was the nearest town that wasn't hit. We were able to jump start two vehicles, and the reserve tank at the local station was untouched. We lucked out. We filled as much as we could and headed back to Emma's and packed up.

We packed up everything including fresh produce, canned products, and the remaining stock in The Hole.

We headed east and aimed for Brookings. Our gas ran low about fifty miles away in the middle of farmland; we had one vehicle that worked. I headed there for help.

Thankfully, they came out for the rest of us. They welcomed us into their small town and were happy about the food we brought. Not that they were short, it was always nice to have more.

The small city of about twelve thousand people had dwindled down to about one thousand. Those who remained were loyal to their town and didn't migrate like the rest of the west.

They honestly believed their remote town would have remained intact, had it not been for the three businessmen who brought the virus into the Holiday Inn.

We've been here about five months now. Making her father proud, Emma registered her agricultural skills with the Twin Falls branch of the Sustainability Project. Her degree, knowledge, and hands on experience was put to work right away. She actually is one of three people that oversee the farming in this division.

Thank God for her skills and a surviving Brooking teenage boy with a stash of marijuana. I won't have to worry about that stutter anymore.

Richie is doing well; he's just being a teenager. Cody is adjusting and is growing at an astronomical rate. Del is the town's weekly entertainment and, like me, will teach at the school when it starts in two weeks.

Recent migration of workers upped the Brookings population. We have forty students.

The United States is restructuring and rebuilding, and, I guess, so is the rest of the world. We don't hear much about the rest of the world. Power is back with limited phone communication and radio. Television and internet are a lost luxury. China, as promised, dropped off shipments of the cure.

I never heard from Edward or Chad again. I can only hope and assume they are doing well.

Things seem to be moving forward but in a different direction. Survival, growth, that seems to be the number one plan.

There is an air of peace that is odd. I can't explain. You wake up every morning, do your thing, and it's peaceful. No tension.

Even though every single person that has survived carries with them memories of the old world, memories of pain, suffering, and loss, we all wear these things proudly like a red badge of courage. It was an experience that brought us to a different place.

In reality, the earth received a cleansing; we have a fresh start. A new beginning, a new world, and a new chance at it all. I hope we do it right this time.

Printed in Great Britain
by Amazon

76724905R00166